BOOK ONE

Mistress of Thieves

CHRONICLES OF A CUTPURSE

CARRIE SUMMERS

MISTRESS OF THIEVES

Cover design by Deranged Doctor Design

Edited by Lindsey Nelson, Exact Edits

ISBN: 1987482050

First Edition: April 2018

10 9 8 7 6 5 4 3 2 1

THE CITY OF OSTGARD

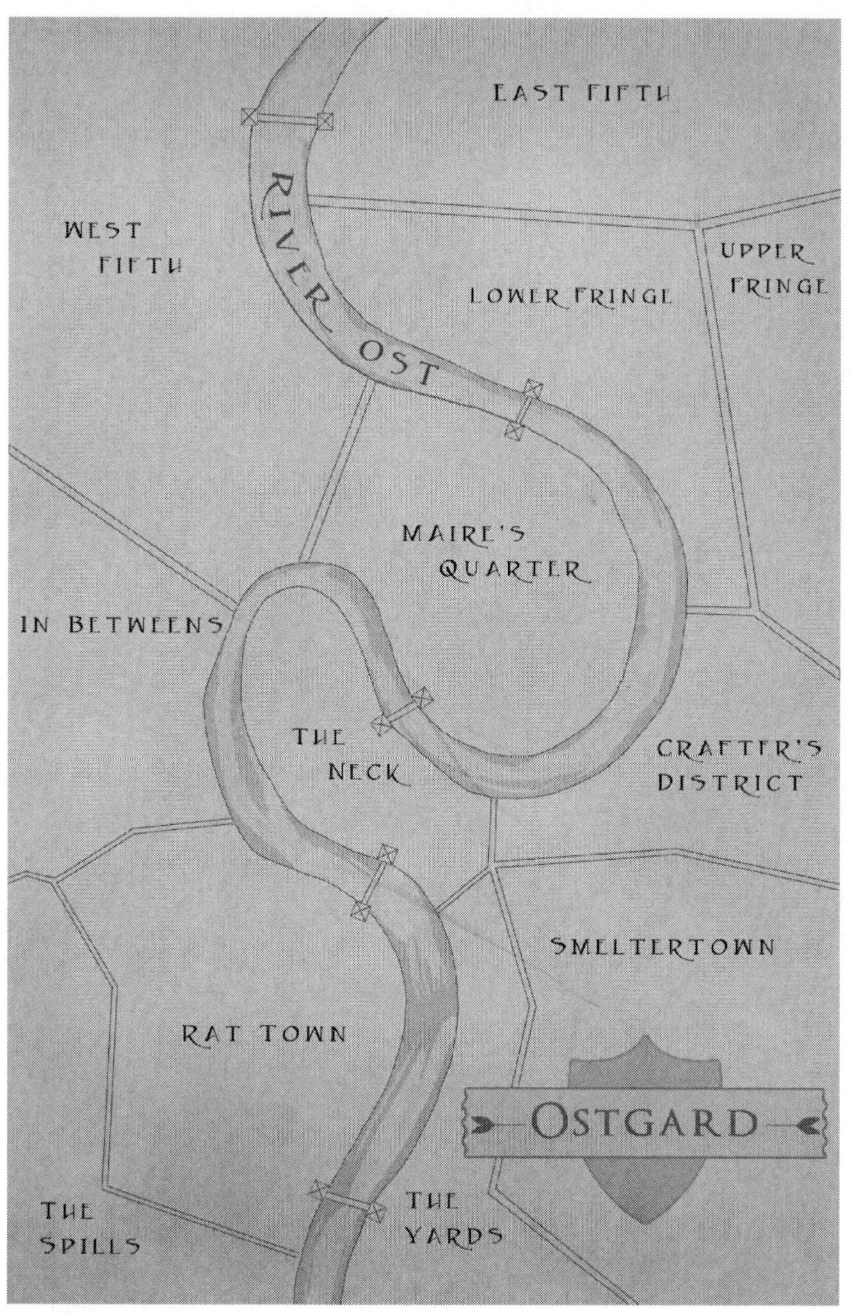

Chapter One

From down in the Spills, Myrrh can't see the rest of the city. Especially on a night like this, when rain falls in a constant hiss against decaying shingles and turns muddy footpaths into shin-deep streams. But she *feels* the vast sprawl of Ostgard lying out there, sodden in the downpour. The hot breath rising from street grates near the waterfront. The panicked shouts of bargemen who tied up too near the Neck, not knowing how storm water turns the River Ost from placid to frothing. Right now, drunks in Rat Town are cursing over dice. Merchants in the West Fifth are trading slave contracts for wine casks.

And somewhere in the city's narrow streets, a man lies dying in a pool of his slowly leaking blood. He might have been a father to her in a different life. In a different port. Far from these cursed alleys and stacked-up stilt houses where grubbers like them have to scratch out what they can.

Hawk was betrayed, and not for the first time. But instead of melting away for a while, he ignored the warnings. The whispers that he spoke too loud for someone of his station, held his head too high. Maybe he'd started to worry about legacy. About leaving behind more than fading memories in those who knew him. Maybe he thought the Queen of Nines owed him a lucky roll or two.

Turns out, his luck was all used up. Everyone knew Hawk's dice had come up sixes when the Scythe, a woman wearing the dull-red uniform of the Maire's personal guard, stalked into his favorite Rat Town tavern and asked for him by name.

After that, it was just a matter of time before they caught him up and dragged him off under dusk's yellow glow. Gone, just like that.

Myrrh wishes she'd cobbled together the courage to say something in the days before. Thanked him for everything he'd taught her, even if he always lectured her against letting emotion show.

The rain seems to beat harder on the slanted roof while she stares out the open door into the dark and the wet. Can't go back now. Nothing will return the old thief to this squat he sometimes shared with her and Nab. His bedroll, shoved in a heap against the far wall, might fetch a bit or two from a rag seller. Enough for a day's bread. He left her that plus the dagger, polished ebony handle and the sharpest edge south of Third Bridge.

She slips a gloved hand to the blade's hilt.

Hawk was more than an aging cutpurse who noticed an urchin girl with a talent for slipping fingers into pockets. He was more than a ratty bedroll abandoned in a run-down stilt shack. He was noble in his own way. A good man who deserved better.

Someone whispered his name in the wrong ears. Myrrh will find out who, and her revenge will be both slow and painful.

But for now, she owes it to Hawk to pack up her grief and focus on the job ahead. People die, but the living still have to eat. Nab's still growing, and even if she could suffer an empty stomach for a couple of days, his eyes are too big beneath that mop of hair as it is.

She slips back into the darkness of the single room and crouches beside Nab's sleeping form. In the darkness, she can't see whether the splotches on his face have faded since he fell asleep crying. Maybe. Maybe he's lost in dreams of better days.

He'd never let her do this when awake, so she kisses the tips of her fingers and presses them to Nab's brow.

"Back later," she whispers.

Myrrh steps into the downpour. She's got work to do tonight.

***

Myrrh hunkers beneath the eaves of the dockmaster's shack, out of the pounding rain. Though, at this point, she can't get any wetter. Her feet slide inside the now-slimy leather of her boots, while the black wool of her tunic clings to her body, twice as heavy and steaming as her skin warms it.

She shivers and squints into the darkness beside the river. Hooded lanterns sputter in the downpour, struggling to push back the night. Down on the water, a bargeman strides his vessel's deck, hunched against the weather. He tugs on the stern line, crouches to add another hitch to the knot, then retreats to the cabin. Candlelight soon leaks from cracks around the tightly shuttered window.

"Hey," a man hisses.

Myrrh whirls, slapping for her blade, then relaxes as she picks Warrell's features from the shadows. Nose hooking to the right from last year's brawl in a dockside tavern. The old scar splitting a dark eyebrow and running white across his weathered cheek. She lowers her hand and turns back toward the water.

"Wasn't sure you'd make it after what happened with Hawk," he says.

Myrrh shrugs. What else was she going to do? Lose tonight's reward and gain herself new enemies? She wishes he hadn't brought up Hawk though. Takes her concentration off the task.

"Second vessel still the target?" she asks.

Warrell moves closer, heat from his body warming her shoulder. "Yeah." He sticks his head past the water streaming off the eaves, then snaps back into the shadows. "No one mentioned landward guards though."

Miser's breath. Myrrh pulls her dagger free of the sheath. Oiled black with only a glint off the razor edge, the blade is as invisible as her thief's garb in the night's dark. Still, she really doesn't want to be in a position where she has to use it. This was supposed to be a quick snatch of a small crate of giftwood carvings, straight off the deck of an anchored barge. Easy.

She sighs. The presence of extra security is probably why the job got kicked down to a pair of freelancers. First Docks, a mass of wooden platforms fastened to the stone quay by rusted bolts and weather-faded rope, is Slivers territory. By rights, they have claim on all pickings. But like most syndicates in Ostgard, they contract out for many reasons. It's up to the grubber offered the job to guess why the rightful owners are passing off much of the profits.

"What do you think?" Warrell asks.

"Gimme a minute."

Myrrh edges around the big man, earning a stream of rainwater down her collar, and rounds the building at the far corner. She slips along the wall, shirt catching on the splintering wood. At the next corner, she peers out, gaining a closer vantage on the unexpected guards. Two men, cloaked against the storm, bracket the ladder that descends to the section of the dock where their target barge is moored.

The guards stare straight ahead, faces in shadow, hands on short swords at their hips. No slouching or leaning against lampposts. No muttering to each other about the weather. Professionals.

Sixes.

She rises onto her toes to try to assess the situation down on the water. The barge is tied close, hiding in the shelter of the stone-built waterfront. Just the top half of the cabin shows, along with some of the tarp-covered stacks of cargo. With guards on the ladder, they'll either have to approach across the maze of docks, jumping between platforms, or—sixes, she hates to think about it on a night like this—they'll have to board the barge from the river.

Though the darkness hides the current's power, the pull only hinted at by the oily glint of lantern light off sinister ripples and curls, the Ost in flood is a dangerous beast. Better to take their chances across the docks and hope the extra sentries don't look down. Of course, that plan doesn't address the possibility of more security on the barge's deck.

As Myrrh shifts backward, one of the guards happens to glance her way. She freezes, pulse hammering. When his motion exposes his face, a chill floods her veins. His eyes lock with hers, drawing forth the silver glint from deep within his gaze.

Glimmer.

She sucks in a breath. The substance was supposed to be a myth. Just a rumor. But if he's using the resin, he can see her as clearly as if she stood in the full glare of the sun.

She closes her eyes and presses back out of his sight. She hasn't done anything yet. No need for the guard to come after her. He has no way to know she planned to pluck that delivery of giftwood on behalf of the Slivers syndicate.

Enough has gone wrong today. Sixes since the sun came up. Best to walk away even if Slivers cuts her out of the running for grubber contracts for a while.

A hand falls on her shoulder. Warrell.

"I'm out," she whispers as she turns back. "Glimmer."

The big man shakes his head, lines of regret on his face. Almost as if he's...apologizing?

"No. You can't." She blinks, unwilling to believe. Five years they've known each other. Introduced by Hawk as fellow independents who understand the perils of freelancing but choose freedom over the shackles of a syndicate.

"Warrell, please."

His face hardens.

Sixes.

Myrrh drops to a crouch to escape his grip. Her boots slip and scrape against rain-wet cobbles as she tries to scramble away. The dagger's still in her hand, the edge that Hawk drew over the whetstone again and again now crunching against stone. A kick to her elbow sends her sprawling, the weapon skittering away into the darkness. Warrell's heavy boot stamps down on her hand. She whines, rolls, and yanks her arm free.

Silver eyes stare down at her. Myrrh blinks against the pouring rain while the guard lays the tip of his sword against her throat, pressing until the metal pierces skin and a drop of warm blood joins the water streaming off her neck. A whine escapes Myrrh's throat as she raises her hands in surrender.

The guard acknowledges Warrell with a curt nod as his partner steps forward to tower over her. The partner reaches into a pocket and pulls out a leather purse. The coins inside scarcely clink as the purse plops into Warrell's hand. Myrrh's throat clamps down. Such a small price for her life. Was this what happened to Hawk too? Sold out for the price of a night's room and board in a midrate flophouse?

Warrell turns to go without another glance.

The glimmer-eyed guard waits until the heavy sounds of Warrell's footsteps are lost within the roar of the rain, then nods to his partner. The other man grabs Myrrh under the armpits and drags her to her feet. Myrrh tries to squirm free, writhing and kicking.

A fist cuffs her on the temple. She sways, dizzied, as a canvas sack drops over her head.

***

The guards lash her wrists with a stiff cord and slip a gag under the sack and between her lips. Myrrh expects to be loaded onto the barge, locked inside the cabin until the vessel unties and ships out. Instead, the guards grab her by the ankles and armpits, grips so tight they might as well be iron, and start walking. The steady rhythm of their footfalls against stone suggests a trip along the waterfront. If they'd ducked into a Rat Town alley or the strip of land where the low streets of the Spills tongue up against the River Ost, she'd expect to hear the thud of boots against earth or the splash as they wade through muck.

A strip of flesh above her belly button is exposed to the rain, and the sodden canvas of the sack clings to her face, sucking into her nostrils with each breath. The longer they walk, the wetter the sack gets until Myrrh is sure she's minutes away from drowning. Just the thought makes her pant with panic, which only sucks more water into her nose. She parts her lips and tries to breathe around the gag. Gets a few sips of precious air, enough to slow her racing pulse.

But when the sound of the river gets louder, rushing on either side as the men carry her onto a bridge—it has to be First Bridge given the distance they've walked—she starts thrashing and flopping like a fish.

Myrrh knows what happens next. They'll lash weight to her ankles. Maybe a sandbag or two—those stay put pretty well. Uncaring hands will grab her up, heave her onto the waist-high wall that keeps frightened mule teams from dragging wagons off the bridge. A shove and she'll fly, her stomach leaping into her throat as the weight of the sandbags flips her feetfirst.

A body thrown off First Bridge won't get caught against the pillars of a downstream span. Not like Fifth Bridge or any of the others in between, where islands of rubble strain all manner of unsightly secrets from the Ost. The Maire won't send a crew to fish out her waterlogged corpse before a delegation arrives from the Inner Kingdoms or the Port Cities. Most likely, the only person who'll really know she's gone—not just moved her squat to another district or another city—will be poor Nab. The kid won't have anyone left to protect him.

It's that thought which gives her the strength to kick free. She yanks a foot out of the slimy leather of her boot, twists her body hard, and rams her leg straight, driving her heel into flesh that gives with a grunt and a whoosh of air out of the man's lungs.

The guard coughs and loses his grip on her other leg.

Her heels smack the stones of the bridge, and she spins, turning facedown and forcing the other guard to cross his wrists and lose his grip on her armpit. Her knees crack the ground. Blind, Myrrh plants a foot and charges forward. She sidesteps by instinct, avoiding a collision with the guard who just lost his grip, and her feet slap the ground, *thud-smack, thud-smack,* as she sprints one-booted down the slope of the arching span.

The thugs shout in frustration. "Miser's breath, this one!"

A weight slams her back as a heavy arm wraps her waist. They go down in a heap, Myrrh's shoulder scraping against rough stone as her tackler's bulk lands atop her. The man pins her with a hand between her shoulder blades, then adds a knee in the small of her back. She can't breathe after the exertion from the run, the panic flooding her body, the weight pressing down and squeezing out the air from her lungs. The sack is too wet, too thick.

A tear leaks from her eye while purple sparks fringe the edges of her vision. Stars explode in her sight as she sucks in vain at the wet fabric over her nose.

For a few heartbeats, her limbs begin to tingle, and then there's an explosion of light. And after, nothing.

Chapter Two

She's not dead, which is better than Myrrh expected. The fog is slow to clear from her thoughts until a violent shiver racks her body and brings her fully awake. She's lying on a cold floor, knobs of her spine pressed against a stone wall. The only sound is the splatter of rain through an open window somewhere near.

She can breathe.

Thank the Nines, the wet sack is gone, replaced by a rough cloth tied tightly over her eyes. It runs across the tender skin where she took the blow to the temple. Whether that is causing the headache or whether it's from earlier damage, she can't be sure.

Myrrh groans through her gag and tries to sit up. Her wrists are still bound, and she winces as she struggles on a floor that's smoother than she first realized. Her head spins as she gets an elbow tucked under her body, and the smell of wet wool from her clothing stuffs her nose.

Somewhere near, a chair squeals against stone. Myrrh freezes, and her strength fails. She wrenches her neck, her elbow slipping out from under her, and the weight of her head slams down.

Footsteps click as someone draws near. They stop just a pace or two away. Close enough that she could reach out her bound wrists and brush the person's ankles. She smells wood smoke, just a hint, and the warm scent of sandalwood. She wants to draw her knees up to protect her belly but resists. Bad enough she's lying helpless before the person's gaze. No need to look more pathetic.

The person inhales, a breath deep enough that she thinks it fills a man's lungs. He exhales, humming faintly and confirming her suspicion with the sonorous note. He walks away, footsteps calm and measured. A rubbing sound, perhaps as he spins on the ball of a foot. She twists her wrists until she can run fingertips over the floor. The tiles are flat but not polished like marble. Slate?

A hinge squeaks, and the sound of the rain is muffled. Metal clicks as he closes the latch on the shutter.

"I'd have seen to your wet clothing already, were it not highly inappropriate to undress you while you were unawares." His voice echoes off the walls, suggesting that—aside from the chair—the room is bare of furnishings and rugs.

Another shiver grips her. Myrrh presses her tongue against the gag, accusations and curses piling up in her throat, but she can't shove the rag past her teeth.

"Of course, you can probably understand why you're still restrained. I needed a chance to speak to you without being kicked in the gut."

Again, the footsteps click while he crosses the room. She counts around fifteen paces before he stops and turns again, likely at the other wall. She guesses the door is opposite her but can't be sure.

She stiffens at the familiar sound of steel leaving a sheath. Again, the footsteps draw near, and a knee pops as the man crouches near her. The tip of the blade drags along the floor, the high-pitched scraping raising hairs on the back of her neck. He touches her, warm fingertips on her right wrist, then slides the blade under the stiff cord binding her hands.

Pressure, enough that he exhales with the effort, and then the rope parts. Blood rushes into her hands, aching as it floods cold fingertips.

"Now please don't attack me," he says mildly. "I truly don't wish to bind you again. A nice dagger, by the way. I had Les retrieve it once my associates finally managed to arrive with you."

Leather creaks as he retreats to a stand. Myrrh slaps her hand against the floor and pushes up, gritting her teeth when dizziness rises. She yanks off the blindfold and winces as light stabs her eyes. Next, she fumbles at the gag, but the strip of cloth is too tight to pull off, and the knot is welded. Eyes narrowed, she snaps her gaze to him while scooting toward the wall for support.

"I was going to suggest that you remove your blindfold, but I see you're good at taking the initiative."

The room's light comes from a massive iron lantern hanging from a chain bolted to the ceiling. The glow of a dozen candles flares behind the man, shadowing his features and silhouetting close-tailored leathers. His hair just touches his ears, rain droplets winking in the light. Judging by his voice and the slightly cocky stance, she guesses he's just a few years older than her. Midtwenties maybe.

Her eyes travel down his arm to where long fingers loosely grip the hilt of Hawk's dagger.

At once, the weight of his death hits her all over again. Her eyes burn as she imagines snatching the blade, whipping it in her grip, and sinking it to the hilt in his neck. It has *not* been a good day.

Unfortunately, her limbs are so stiff she doubts she could even reach her feet, much less stay on them.

"If you'll permit me...?" he asks, stepping close and pointing at her ear with the blade.

Her brows draw together until she realizes he means the gag. Swallowing her pride, she nods.

He drops to a crouch on one heel, the other leg splayed out before her, then slips a finger under the gag to guide his other hand. The candlelight strikes his face as he cocks his head in concentration. Dark eyes, straight brow. They're features common among Ostgarders with roots in the eastern mountains. She's definitely never seen him before.

The threads in the gag part with a tearing sound. As it loosens and falls from her mouth, she rejects a dozen threats that form in her mind. A sharp tongue won't earn her anything. Instead, she swallows the taste of linen, purses her lips, and contemplates spitting at the man. Probably not a good idea either.

"Water?" he asks.

She fights the impulse to reject the offer and nods instead. Thirst will only make her weak. Sheathing Hawk's dagger, the man stands and moves aside, granting a better view of the room. As she suspected, a single straight-backed chair stands near a door that hangs ajar. The walls are unadorned stone, broken only by one shuttered window. Beyond the door, the corridor is dim but not dark. The man crosses the room with long strides, moving with the grace of the thief she suspects he is. If he were part of the Shield Watch, the city guard that keeps violence in Ostgard to a mere simmer, she'd either be in a Smeltertown prison or strung up from the gibbet overhanging the Ost south of First Bridge. If he worked under the Scythe, he'd wear red, and she'd be cooling in an alley beside Hawk.

But he doesn't bear any of the obvious marks of the city's major criminal syndicates either. No bar piercing the cartilage of his upper ear like the Slivers, no gray scarf around his knee like Haven favors. Maybe the simple explanation is he's security for the merchant group that controls the barge she was planning to rob. It's possible the owners want to know who sent her. But then, how does she explain Warrell's betrayal? He had the same information she did, and he'd clearly been cooperating with the guards on the barge.

The man sticks his head into the hallway, speaks in a low voice, and soon returns with a tin cup of water. He nods toward the floor near her hip. Myrrh's surprised to see a neatly folded stack of clothes beside a pair of dry boots.

"They should fit," he says as he places the cup near her knee. "I'll give you privacy to change. Please don't do something stupid like trying to escape out the window. The drop is farther than you want to fall, and a downclimb in this rain would not go well."

"Am I a prisoner?" she asks as he walks to the door. She's thinking of Nab waking alone in their miserable squat. Losing two people in less than a day.

His gaze is piercing, but she can't read the expression on his face. "We'll speak more once you're dressed."

Chapter Three

Myrrh's knees wobble as she crosses the room, clad and dry. She can't let him see how weak she is, so she locks her knees before she nudges the door open.

Though someone was in the hallway earlier to hand him the cup of water, now the man is alone. He leans a shoulder against more bare-stone walls and has his feet crossed easily at the ankles. Whereas the first room smelled mostly of rain and wet stone, the corridor carries that same sandalwood scent she smelled on his clothing. Candles flicker in glass lanterns tinted a faint ruby. A runner woven with patterns of Ishvar design stretches the length of the hall, softening the slate tiles and swallowing the echoes.

She spots a window partway down the hall. It's still dark outside. Still night. Maybe Nab is still asleep.

The man keeps his hands in his pockets as he pushes off the wall. "I have a fire going in one of the other rooms."

Myrrh remains in the doorway. "Why am I here?"

"I prefer not to answer questions out of order."

"And I prefer knowing why I was betrayed by my friend and carried off like a sack of oats."

His face hardens. "The disloyalty of your associates is not something I can speak to. Perhaps you should choose your allies more carefully. As for your treatment, it was...necessary. Your friend needed to believe he'd thrown you to the hounds. Now, I'm offering a warm fire and a chance to speak on respectful terms. Or will you force me to reconsider my hospitality?"

He makes a point of running his eyes down her length. She can't deny that the clothing is some of the most comfortable she's worn. Finespun linen moves over her skin with none of the scratchiness of wool, and the cut allows as much movement as her thief's garb. Even the boots are a passable fit, new leather not yet scuffed with use. The dyes on the shirt and trousers are a mix of midnight blues and steel gray, while the boots are a deep red that few can impart to leather.

Hardening her jaw, she forces herself to keep her gaze off the floor as she strides forward. With a nod, he turns and leads the way.

At the window, he slows and swings a shutter closed, but not before Myrrh notices the shine of a real glass pane and—far below—the flicker of streetlamps struggling against the night and the storm. They must be three floors up, maybe four. How far did his men carry her? Well away from Rat Town and its crowd of ramshackle buildings that can't grow taller than a couple stories without the lower supports bowing out and splintering.

Before the corridor ends in a staircase that turns a sharp corner into darkness, she feels the heat radiating from an open door on the left. The man stops at the threshold and waves her in.

The room is as bedecked as the first chamber was bare. Deep carpets overlap on the floor, a mix of reds that swallow her feet and make her want to slip off her boots. Three large chairs upholstered in leather and set with pillows circle a blazing fire. Atop a low wood table polished to a gleam, a decanter of burgundy wine waits beside a pair of goblets.

The man adjusts a painting as he steps toward a chair near the wall. He waits, arms crossed, until she sits in the chair farthest away from him. With a sigh and a smirk, he steps forward and takes the central seat.

"I prefer not to yell across the room. Wine?"

He picks up a goblet and the decanter. When Myrrh shakes her head, he shrugs and returns both to the table.

The man holds her stare while the fire crackles. She gets the sense he's searching for something in her expression. Maybe he's waiting for her to break down. She keeps her emotions off her face just like Hawk taught her.

"Hawk spoke of you often." The faint narrowing of his eyes shows a smugness over dropping this surprise.

A vein pulses in her temple. Can he see it? She blinks as if he hadn't spoken.

With a sigh, the man reaches for the wine. He splashes a small measure into a goblet and sips, running the liquid over his tongue before swallowing. "A nice vintage. Among other things, this cask came from the barge you meant to rob."

Does that mean he represents the vessel's owners after all? She really doesn't think so. Maybe he swiped the score out from under her...that might explain the guards on the waterfront. Extra muscle standing watch while he grabbed what he wanted.

"What makes you think I had plans for that barge?"

He returns the goblet to the table. "Perhaps an introduction is in order. I'm Glint."

"Seems you already know plenty about me. Or at least, you assume to."

"But the exchange of monikers is a social custom. It puts the other person at ease by permitting them to freely use something which is deeply and personally your own. In many cases, your very first and only permanent possession."

She thinks she detects a hint of amusement in his eyes. "And Glint is the name your mother gave you?"

The corner of his mouth draws back in a wry smile. "As much as Myrrh was yours, I assume." He inhales deeply and closes his eyes as if scenting the heady incense she chose to name herself after. "Pungent. A touch exotic. And very, very smooth. It's a decent choice."

"Perhaps more inventive than...what? The flash of a blade in the night?"

"Is that where you think I got the name?" He stretches his legs out long, pointing the soles of his boots toward the fire. "I prefer to imagine the winking of lots and lots of coins under candlelight."

"Well, Glint, we've met. Now why am I here?"

As he draws his feet back and leans forward, his posture changes from lazy cat to ready predator. She suddenly feels as if there's an invisible blade at her throat. A wrong word and he'll press the edge through flesh.

"You're here because Hawk trusted you. That's enough to earn you an audition. But don't mistake your position. It takes more than the word of a dead man to convince me of your worth."

An *audition*? What could possibly make him think she'd want that?

"I don't even know who you are."

He circles his hand in the air. "Which is why I proposed we begin with the introductions, a process that didn't seem to interest you."

She narrows her eyes, done being polite. Whatever power this man thinks he has over her, she'd rather face a contest of blades than sit here dueling with words. "When Hawk spoke of me, did he mention that I hate arrogant thieves who pretend at thrones and castles by collecting sycophants and vying for so-called territory in a city that belongs to no one but the Maire and those who pay his tariffs?"

A wide grin splits Glint's face. "He may have mentioned something of the sort." Rotating toward the table, he pours himself another small measure of wine. "You sure you won't have some?"

Myrrh doesn't answer.

He sighs and leans back, hand wrapped around the goblet's globe. "So, given the information at hand, you've decided I'm a thief. Interesting."

"I shouldn't have been so precise. Smuggler or extortionist are equally likely. Certainly, you're an abductor, though you'll make no ransom on someone like me."

He swirls the wine in his glass, watching the flames. "In truth, I'd rather be none of those things. But I refuse to follow rules designed to prevent me from achieving more in life than a sore back and daily meals. So I suppose I'll accept your label, though I'd prefer to consider myself an entrepreneur. Or perhaps a even a rebel."

"How did you know Hawk?"

"So you admit he was familiar to you."

"You seem to know enough about me there's little point in pretending. And 'familiar' would be an understatement."

When he glances at her, his eyes hold real pain. “Hard to speak of him in the past, isn’t it?”

She surprises herself by speaking honestly. “It’s not the words that hurt. Words lie as often as they speak truth. It’s the absence. The space he used to fill.”

If she’s not mistaken, a faint light dies in Glint’s eyes as he lowers them from her face. “You really believe it, then? Don’t you think there’s a chance the Scythe was merciful?”

“Six blades came with her to take him down. That’s not the sort of force she uses when she plans to have a chat.”

He swigs the contents of his goblet in a single swallow and pours another. “No, I know he’s gone. I just hope I can keep from letting his dreams die with him.”

What dreams? She runs a hand down the fine weave of her trousers, trying to ignore the tightness in her chest. She thought Hawk trusted her. Sometimes, she even imagined he considered her something of a daughter. Yet she knew nothing of his interaction with this man.

“You still haven’t answered my question. How did you know him?”

He shoots her a sideways glance. “We had...joint interests. As far as the details go, you still have to earn my trust, remember?”

“Right. Your *audition*. Didn’t Hawk tell you I’m freelance? I’m not looking for any permanent affiliation. But if you have a contract, I’ll consider it.”

A sad smile touches his lips. “You can’t go back, you know. That was the whole point of nabbing you under that other grubber’s nose. As far as Rat Town is concerned, you need to be as dead as Hawk.

Or at least taken by the bargeman you tried to rob, likely to be sold in a slave market downriver."

"What? Why?" Again her thoughts shoot to Nab, sleeping alone in the run-down shack in the Spills. She *has* to go back.

"Though I hope my efforts in saving you will benefit me directly, I had you plucked off the waterfront because Hawk asked it of me. If the worst happened, he knew you'd be next. Someone around Rat Town didn't like the work Hawk and I were doing."

"Another reason for me to get back. Hawk deserves vengeance."

"And where will you start? Do you plan to take on the Slivers gang alone? You saw where your grubber friend's—"

"Warrell."

"You saw where Warrell's true loyalties lie. The moment you lost Hawk's protection, he sold you straight off. Granted, he sold you to me. But it could as easily have been the next group that came asking."

"There's someone in the Spills who depends on me. I can't just leave him."

"The kid. Nab."

Her fingertips tingle with sudden panic. She shouldn't have mentioned the boy. Not without knowing more about Glint's intentions. For all she really knows, this is an elaborate ruse. Or is she just being paranoid?

"Myrrh, I won't hurt him. I swear it."

She meets his eyes. Searches for clues.

"I'll get him to safety. Please don't risk yourself. I owe it to Hawk to keep you safe from his enemies."

She takes a deep breath. His tone is honest, but thieves are consummate liars.

"Would you at least accept my hospitality for tonight?" he asks. "This...base of operations is still coming together, as you may have noticed by the lack of furnishings. And I must warn you—I'm not much of a cook. Safer for you to just stick with bread and cheese for now."

She shakes her head, confused. "You had a servant fetch the water, didn't you? Not that I care about the meal."

He smirks. "I had Les fetch the water, and once I decided I could handle you if you got a notion to pick a fight, I sent him away. As for my cook, he'll be back tomorrow. I sent him to safety in case you reacted poorly to my offer and tried to cut your way to freedom."

Is he trying to distract her by joking? Put her at ease? Something doesn't add up here. Myrrh taps fingers on her knees. Most criminal enterprises have a strict pecking order where the higher-ups don't fend for themselves in empty buildings. "Which syndicate?"

"Come again?"

"If I'm going to be knifed in my sleep, I want to know which organization bears responsibility. Who do you work for?"

He raises a single eyebrow. "I thought it was obvious."

"I know all the major players, but you don't wear a mark."

"Not that. I don't *work for* anyone. Now, is there an organization that answers to me? Perhaps. But you won't have heard of us."

More vague answers. She sighs. All at once, the night's events seem to press down. Myrrh's body is heavy with grief and confusion. She *does* need rest, even if she leaves at first light to find Nab.

"Come on," he says. "I'll find you a room with enough furniture you won't have to sleep on the floor. One you can bar from the inside if you wish."

He offers a hand, which she reluctantly takes. Calluses ridge his palm, but his nails are neatly filed. As soon as she's upright, she jerks her hand away.

With a nod of understanding, he leads her out the door.

Chapter Four

Myrrh wakes with a start, disoriented. There are no splintered floorboards under her cheek. No familiar warbling of water birds in the bog at the district's edge. She sits bolt upright and throws off a feather-stuffed coverlet.

And nearly falls off the thigh-high bed.

She coughs and grabs handfuls of the sheet. Last night's events come roaring back.

She's in Glint's safe house. Or rather, as he called it, his base of operations. Whatever it is, she's not in immediate danger. At least, she's safe enough that she can calm her thudding heart and panting breaths.

The slate floors cool the bottoms of her feet while she shuffles to the window. Midmorning sun and the sound of carts and voices pour into the room when she opens the shutters. No glass here; the outside air smells like roasting meat, still-wet pavement, and the bird droppings from a nest wedged in a stone cornice above the window. With a deeper inhalation, she even catches acrid whiffs from Smeltertown.

The window faces roughly east. Leaning her head and shoulders out, she searches for the glint of sunlight off the River Ost. The men last night carried her across First Bridge to the east bank of the river, which would probably put her in the wrong place to see the water from an east-facing window. Still, just because she can't see the river doesn't mean she has a sixing clue about her location. The buildings across the street could be hiding a view of Fifth Bridge for all she knows.

Actually, that's not true. If she were next to Fifth Bridge, she'd probably be bathing in diamonds and toweling off with Tulpan silk. Or at the very least, she wouldn't notice soot stains on the stonework across the street. And the street would be three times as wide. And sure as the Miser's greed, there wouldn't be a beggar on the street corner to the right. Missing a lower leg, the man jiggles a cup at passersby.

Over rooftops in that direction, thick haze hides the view. Most likely, that's Smeltertown, stewing in its own mess. Unless the wind has shifted, throwing smog over Rat Town or even up to In Betweens.

Basically, she wouldn't bet three coppers on her guess at a location. She claps the shutter closed and pads to the door.

Myrrh smirks as the bar lifts from its housing easily; last night she was so exhausted, the weight of the smooth hardwood plank was almost too much for her grip. She lowers it to the floor one-handed before tugging the door open.

Silence echoes in the hallway. She peers at the other doors, each closed and uninviting. Before bed, Glint led her down just one flight of steps, which means the sitting room is one floor up. Seems the best place to start looking for him. She heads for the stairwell.

"Down here."

She jumps when his voice floats up the stairs from somewhere below. How did he hear her padding barefoot on smooth stone?

Which reminds her...she glances down at her feet. Only a fool gets caught wearing shoes—or lack thereof—she can't run in.

"Forgot something," she calls.

"You won't need shoes until after breakfast."

Seriously, how did he know? Myrrh shakes her head and goes back for her boots anyway.

On the next floor down, a locked door bars passage off the landing. With a shrug, Myrrh keeps descending. The stairs end at a wide archway that opens into a dining room. Glint sits at a long wood table, polished like the one upstairs. Half-a-dozen chairs would fit easily at each side. Right now, there are only two.

A wheel of cheese stands directly on the polished wood. Glint hasn't bothered with plates, but he's brought out a basket of fruit and a paring knife. He has a foot propped on the other chair, but at her approach, he sits up straight and nudges the chair out with his toe.

"Where's Nab?" she asks.

"On his way. We're moving cautiously to throw off pursuit."

"How soon?"

"By tonight."

He pulls Hawk's dagger from the sheath, looks at the cheese, then runs a finger down the oiled blade. After examining the residue on his fingertip, he shakes his head and sets the blade aside.

Next to her place at the table.

As she sits, she lays a hand on the hilt, recalling last night's desire to steal the dagger and use it to slit his throat. He raises an eyebrow when she meets his gaze.

"I got the feeling you don't like the word *audition*. My apologies. But if I'm going to learn to trust you, we must start somewhere."

She pats her hip, feeling for the dagger's sheath. But of course, it's not there. Her belt, along with her dark woolens, is probably still in the upstairs room where she woke. She settles for moving the blade out of his reach.

Glint draws a long knife from his belt and sets it beside the fruit. Just out of *her* reach.

"But since we haven't yet established that trust, I'd like to prepare for an even fight," he says with a smirk.

She gets the sense that he doesn't really believe the fight would be even. He's too arrogant to accept the idea that he might lose.

"Where are we?" she asks. "And if you don't want me reaching toward your weapon, please pass the fruit."

He slides the basket toward her. "Which district, you mean? Lower Fringe."

A long way from home. Glint's men had to have carried her for at least two hours to get here. More if they used the thieves' paths for secrecy. That's way too long for her to have remained unconscious after fainting in a panic to get air.

She fixes him with a hard stare. "What did you drug me with?"

"I regret the necessity."

"I still want an answer."

"Nightbark. As long as you avoid another dose within the next seven days, you'll be fine."

She grabs an apple and sinks her teeth into the crisp flesh. Tart juice floods her mouth as she chews. Nightbark is difficult to acquire. But it's not nearly as rare—or expensive, she imagines—as glimmer. Glint has resources. More than she would guess based on the half-furnished state of this place.

"Lower Fringe isn't the most likely spot for your sort of work," she comments.

"*Our* sort of work. Don't pretend you're any different. And yes, it's a strange choice with so much Shield presence, especially around this area of the district."

"Which area is that?"

He jabs a thumb over his shoulder, toward the back wall. "Fourth Bridge is about a block that way."

Fourth Bridge. The main access to Maire's Quarter from anywhere east of the River Ost. The captain of the Shield Watch lines guardsmen shoulder to shoulder across the span. More defend the Lower Fringe waterfront, standing stone-faced every few paces. Only a lunatic would base a criminal operation a block from that many city guardsmen. Which apparently, Glint is.

"Why should I believe you about Nab?"

He smiles, amused. "You know, he's almost as feisty as you. Kicked one of my men in a rather unpleasant place."

"I'd like proof you have him."

"Later."

"Why not now?"

"Because I'm eating breakfast, and I've asked my associates to stay away so that we could speak in peace. I said I'd take care of it, and I have." A harsh edge has entered his voice.

Myrrh takes another bite of her apple as she shrugs a shoulder. Whether it angers him or not, she won't act like the meek child he seems to expect. She chews in silence while Glint toys with the paring knife. After a moment, he pulls the cheese close, leaving a wide smudge on the polished table, and starts cutting out a small wedge.

"Be a shame to scar your tabletop."

He casts her a sideways glance. "I may not know how to cook, but I *am* rather good with a knife."

True to his word, the piece of cheese comes away clean. No scratches mar the table.

"I'm curious: did they build the walls around the table, or did you hire a woodworker to construct the table right here? Clearly it didn't fit through the door."

He smirks. "It was here when I bought the place. You'll just have to choose your own answer. Cheese?"

"Please."

As he hands over a creamy white wedge, he meets her eyes. "I'd like to get down to business if you don't mind."

She raises a brow in invitation.

"Today, you'll take an allowance of coin and purchase a few items. You need more pockets in your work clothes. Something with a better hood, but not a cloak. Wool is okay for reconnaissance, but you need leather for defense on any close work."

Myrrh holds tight to her anger, though the condescension makes her fingers itch to snatch her dagger.

His eyes flick to the blade she's thinking of drawing across his throat. "I assume you've already trained with blades that length. I'll find time over the coming days to help with the rapier and"—he glances at her arm and shoulder—"short sword if you have the grip for it."

She can't help shaking her head. "You're still acting like I *want* to be your underling. And for that matter, like I need your instruction."

He taps a finger on the table. "Pressing matters have made me abrupt. I apologize for that. But listen, Myrrh. I have plans that I'd like to make you part of. Work that Hawk and I began together."

"Plans that you won't tell me about."

"Not yet."

"I've always been freelance."

"And you've spent your life building a network of contacts, safe houses, and stashes. I get it. But that's gone now. You have to start over. I'd like to humbly offer that you'd do well to start over with me."

"I don't get the sense you do anything 'humbly.'"

He chuckles. "Maybe not. Leading men and women twice my age has forced me to project confidence."

"Anyway, I should accept all this on your word alone?"

"Don't forget the evidence. What was his name? Warrell? Plus, I'm bringing Nab to you."

Her apple is down to a lumpy core dangling from the stem. She holds it up to question what she should do with it.

"Leave it. Someone will deal with it later."

With a shrug, she drops it on the polished tabletop. Droplets of juice splatter.

"If I take your money and go shopping, I'll be in debt. I don't like that."

"What if I call it a gift?"

"I like charity even less."

"Then do a job for me tonight. As payment. Worst case, you'll have worked your first contract outside of Rat Town. No different than freelancing, but in this case, you have the option to consider a longer-term arrangement."

She plucks her piece of cheese from the table. It's nutty, smooth on her tongue. Idly running a finger along her dagger's hilt, she taps a foot and thinks.

"I'll consider the job but only after I see Nab."

"Fair."

She holds out her hand. "I'll need a purse I can keep under my tunic."

Chapter Five

The first leatherworker raises an eyebrow at her request for pockets sewn inside the sleeves and along the ribs of a jacket. Myrrh ignores his reaction and fingers a thick belt with three buckles that fasten in the front. It's sized for a man.

"And something like this," she says. "But add a second sheath on the opposite hip."

"You want all this today?" He glances around the shop as if to draw her attention to the half-finished work on the forms.

"If you want my business."

His lip twitches, but he agrees. Nice thing about Crafter's Row: there are a dozen or more tradespeople per specialty. Makes for a nice buyers' market, especially when the client offers discretion when it comes to whether the seller sets aside coin for the Maire's taxes.

She picks a different shop to order trousers. It's just better not to be *too* memorable.

Clouds thicken over the city after midday, and a light drizzle begins to fall. Myrrh buys a cloak because she's tired of being wet but adds a woolen undershirt with a tight-fitting hood because Glint asked for it. Afterward, she traces a winding route through the streets, passing in and out of the southern portion of Lower Fringe to familiarize herself with the lay of this part of the city. Her eyes pick out darker alcoves, loose sewer grates, and plank bridges that cross from rooftop to rooftop. Like in every part of the city, the thieves' paths crisscross the territory. An ever-shifting network of tunnels, alleys, bridges, and open windows that provide unseen passage for Ostgard's underworld. If the situation hasn't changed since she last heard, Porcelain Hand controls the territory around Lower Fringe and Crafter's Row. They likely have urchins watching entrances to the paths, collecting tolls from nonmembers in good standing, raising the alarm if an enemy draws near.

Myrrh needs no access to the paths today. The small reputation she had with the Shields in Rat Town and the Spills is nothing here. And besides, she doubts a Shield would recognize her now. The fine weave and precise hems of her linen clothes give the appearance of a respectable citizen, even if her sheathed dagger makes her look overly cautious.

Around the time evening adds a dirty glow to the drizzling mist, she fetches her purchases, haggling a bit because she can. No one else is going to buy the finished items—at least not right away—and the makers will still earn nearly half again their usual rate if they don't pay the Maire's taxes.

She pulls the cloak tight as she winds her way back into Lower Fringe, the cobbled streets closing in tight while the buildings rise tall and block out the sky. Merchants and clerks, those who can't afford a mansion farther north or in Maire's Quarter, shuffle home with heads bowed. Hawkers open oiled canopies over their displays, crying out offers on kitchen knives and bundled flowers, sweet buns and offerings for the Patron's shrine. With a blade at her hip, most passersby give Myrrh a wide berth.

But not a big man with work-hardened knuckles and an ugly grin. He smells like liquor and jabs an elbow into her shoulder when she refuses to step out of his way as others on the street do.

Myrrh curls her lip at his reek, the stench of Ost water soaking the cuffs of his pants, body odor and the smell of sweat coming from his pores. He likely works the docks, and from the particular hint of sewage, she guesses it's First Docks rather than Third. The smell of the Ost gets progressively worse as the water flows through the city from Fifth Bridge and under three more to the bridge and docks where she ran into trouble last night. Below First Bridge, it's sometimes so foul with runoff from the Smeltertown slag heaps that the water stings the skin. She doesn't even want to think about what would happen to someone who fell in.

The man walks sideways as he looks back at her. Just waiting for her to challenge. Maybe he ran into trouble, lost his wages. Maybe that's why he's a couple hours walk from First Docks. Back in Rat Town, she would have put him down with a couple swift kicks, a duck under a swipe aimed at her head, maybe a dagger strike deep enough to sting but not to kill. Not here. Not until she sees Nab and knows he's okay.

She shakes her head and keeps walking. Back to Glint and the work she owes him tonight.

***

When Myrrh steps through the front door into the dining room, Nab lowers the turkey leg he's gnawing. His look demands that she *not* come rushing over like he's some little kid in need of a mother. Even though he is. But with Glint hanging out by the front windows, inspecting heavy brocade curtains that have replaced the shutters that were there this morning, Nab doesn't want to show it.

Wasn't *that* long ago, maybe eight years, that she felt the same way. An urchin holding too tight to a gift of stale bread, narrowing her eyes to pretend she was just as hardened as the crooks and smugglers that clung to Hawk like a life raft in those days. Before Slivers moved into Rat Town and swallowed up the work.

She grants Nab his wish, acknowledging him with a nod rather than the hug she wants to wrap him in. Her next breath is easier to take. The kid's alive. She owes Glint for that.

"A cloak," Glint comments.

Myrrh shuts the heavy door, muffling the sounds from the street. "Because I'm sick of getting rained on. But I also got this. Just like you ordered." She pulls the hooded tunic from a canvas sack she bought to hold her other purchases. The wool is dark. Not *quite* black, but it won't make much difference for night work. She holds it by the shoulders, shaking the garment until he smirks and nods.

"Have you eaten?" he asks. "Good to fill your stomach before heading out. I plan to send you on an errand into the night market on the Neck—you'll want to cross Maire's Quarter to get there."

Myrrh's steps stutter as she approaches the table. True, Maire's Quarter and the Neck are twin peninsulas made by a sweeping S curve in the River Ost. The juts of land wrap around one another like a pair of fish, each chasing the other's tail. Someone with the proper papers and a respectable bearing could easily cross Fourth Bridge into Maire's Quarter, and from there, cross Third Bridge to reach the Neck and its night market. But she's neither respectable nor blessed with paperwork bearing the Maire's seal.

Of course from here, it would take three times as long to reach the night market by other paths. But thieves just *don't* stroll beneath the Maire's nose.

Nab sets his nearly stripped turkey leg directly on the table and yawns as he stands. Myrrh cringes, feeling strangely responsible for his bad manners. Then she remembers how Glint eats and shrugs. The mess from breakfast has already been polished away. No doubt the same will happen tonight.

"You seem hesitant," Glint says. She can't see his features because of evening light falling through the window behind him, but she senses his smirk.

"No, you're right. Maire's Quarter is the best route."

Nab makes a little shocked noise. She glares at him for doubting.

"Well then," Glint says, "since you won't need extra time to hike all the way around, perhaps we should have a *proper* dinner. We can discuss tonight's work while we eat."

He strides across the room and kicks a door. Moments later, a red-cheeked man pokes his head out and nods in response to Glint's low request. A boy scurries out with a rag, straightens the chairs—there are three now—and wipes down the table, carrying away the turkey leg. He then hurries back through the door and returns with a square tablecloth and a pair of candlesticks. Once laid out and held down by the candles, the cloth covers just a third of the table, but the gold-thread embroidery speaks to the cost.

Myrrh doesn't realize she's taken a surprised step back until her heel catches on the edge of a slate tile.

Glint's eyes hold a spark of amusement as he grabs a candle from a wall sconce and uses it to light the wicks on the delicate tapers. He pulls out a chair for her, gestures for Nab to sit back down, and takes his spot at the head of the table.

The boy returns again, bearing a stack of fine china and polished silver cutlery. A set of napkins drapes his arm. As he sets the table, he casts a shy glance at her and a somewhat sullen one at Nab—they're near the same age, and the boy no doubt wonders what Nab has done to earn a seat at Glint's table.

After a carafe of wine arrives, Glint snaps the folds from his napkin and places it on his lap. He pours a swallow each for Myrrh and himself, then summons a glass of water for Nab.

He raises his glass. "To friends among scoundrels."

Chapter Six

Glint meets her in a dark corridor under the stairs, next to a narrow door. Myrrh's new leathers fit close to her skin, making her feel stronger. Quicker.

"What do you know about glimmer?" he asks, holding up a little packet of waxed paper.

"I know your men used it to capture me."

"Anything else?"

"I thought it was just a rumor. Rat Town grubbers say it makes you twice as strong. Along with the ability to see in pitch darkness. A miracle for thieves, which is why I was sure it didn't exist."

A wry smile tugs the corner of his mouth. "I worked hard to connect with a source. It's...few sellers want to traffic in something that can be so dangerous if used wrong. But if rumors—and misinformation—are spreading, I worry that our access will make us a target."

He catches her wrist, turns her palm face up, and drops the packet into her hand. A small ball of dark resin has been pressed into the paper.

"It won't make you stronger. Just...quicker. More precise. Your grubber friends are right about the changes to your vision, mostly. Glimmer-sight is much like a cat's. Your eyes will amplify the faintest hints of light. Of course, bright light is painful when under the influence."

"What's the danger in misuse?"

"Nothing if the dose is precise and the resin uncontaminated. It comes from the same distant island as nightbark, which you have recent experience with. The compounds from Haava have impressive effects, but if too much of any particular resin gets into one's body, there can be permanent damage. No more than one dose every five days, okay?"

Myrrh tucks the packet into a pocket inside her jacket. Near her left collarbone. The little lump of resin seems to push on the nerves there.

"What kind of damage?"

"Depends on the compound. I haven't seen it for myself, but I've heard the silver gleam never leaves the eyes of the glimmer-blind. That's how you recognize them. Plus their inability to see in daylight. Sunlight turns their vision pure white and painful. Which is why, on the source island, they're sometimes called Whites."

"So who measured this dose?"

He nods. "Good. Better to be cautious. It was portioned by my supplier."

"And I should trust this person?"

"As much as you can anyone. She has a long history of providing the resin to royal houses in the Inner Kingdoms. The personal guard and assassins working for the Sapphire Queen reportedly use it frequently. I was able to verify the contracts between the palaces and my contact, though I can't confirm the use by the Sapphire guard. The throne holds its secrets too close."

"Do *you* take her word on the correctness of the doses?"

He smirks. “Yes, but I also cut each ball in half. The effects are shorter-lived than would technically be safe, but I have no desire to see my associates go glimmer-blind.”

Myrrh lays her hand on the deadbolt securing the door. “I should go.”

He steps back and bows. “I won’t keep you from your task. Don’t fear to use the resin if circumstances demand. I’d like it if you returned alive.”

***

Down near the river, Myrrh rolls her shoulders, rises onto the balls of her feet, takes a deep breath.

The night wraps her, an old friend. Wherever the work, whatever the job, she can count on darkness to help her.

Ahead, the waterfront curves a graceful arc, bending away from her in either direction. Fourth Bridge arches over the water, the guardhouse in the center blazing with light. The Shield Watch is out in force, just like she expected. No boon from the Queen of Nines tonight.

The bridge is a big problem. From this part of the city, it’s the only access to Maire’s Quarter. She can’t cross it openly. At this time of night, delivery carts are prohibited, so she can’t stow away. A merchant’s entourage would need to present papers for every member—she has slim chances of impersonating someone with rightful access.

This is a test. She and Glint both know it.

A few wagons and horseback riders travel along the waterfront, wheels squealing and animals snorting. Myrrh blends with the flow of pedestrians as she heads north, checking for gaps in the guards' attention. Every Shield stands rigid with keen eyes.

She stops near a spill of light from an upscale tavern. Inside, men in waistcoats sip brandy. Women titter over rose-colored wine. Myrrh steps back a few paces and peers down a narrow aisle between the tavern and the neighboring building. Back in the darkness, a short staircase leads to a side door in the tavern. Probably the kitchen entrance. She slips into the slender corridor to wait and watch, ears perked for the sound of a door opening behind her.

On the section of river ahead, a pair of barges cut dark shadows over the water. Men work long poles on one, shoving the vessel upriver. On the other, two men in the stern slice the water with sleek paddles, guiding the barge down the slow-flowing river. It's a different scene than First Bridge, where captains use sails and oar teams for both directions of travel. Here, the passages beneath Fourth Bridge are barely wide enough to allow the vessels through. Poles are the only way to move upriver.

She studies the cadence of the pole men. Eight on a side. They work in groups to the shout of a man in the rear of the barge. With each barked command, half the men hold the vessel in place while the others move forward and plant their poles to pull the heavy barge forward. The process seems agonizingly slow.

At the head of the vessel, a spotter holds a lantern high, watching the inky water for bobbing flotsam. Which makes Myrrh think. If the barge were swept downstream to collide with the bridge, the chaos might be enough to let her slip across to Maire's Quarter unnoticed. She chews her lip, then shakes her head. Innocent people might get hurt. And crashing a barge is hardly a low-profile tactic; she expects Glint is interested in her ability to be discreet.

Not that she cares what he thinks. This job is payback for the coin and Nab's rescue.

Behind her, the door squeaks as it opens. Smoothly, so as not to attract attention, Myrrh slips out of the aisle. Liquid splashes, and she peeks around the corner in time to see the cook shaking the last drops of water from a pot.

Myrrh stiffens when she peers into the recesses of the corridor. The aisle dead-ends against the back wall of another building, and in the glow from the door, she picks out a darker shadow against the stone blocks. Medium height, slight build. Another thief?

The door clicks shut, snuffing the last light. Leather scuffs against stone. A faint grunt comes from above, and she whips her head up to see a shadow disappearing over the edge of the rooftop.

How long was the person behind her? She hates to think they slipped down from the rooftop without her knowing. Maybe they entered the aisle when the cook opened the door.

Maybe it was Glint keeping tabs.

She runs a thumb over the little lump of glimmer inside her jacket. It probably *was* him, now that she considers it.

Fine. Let him follow her, as long as he doesn't mess up her job.

The presence of another shadowy figure reminds her of the thieves' paths she noticed during the day. The paths web the city from Fifth Bridge down to First. Why assume that Maire's Quarter is different?

If anything, hidden access is *more* critical when it comes to the Quarter. And if thieves and smugglers can't go over Fourth Bridge, could it be they go under?

***

The entrance is a loose grate a block and a half away from the bridge. It opens inside an alley just a few doors away from Glint's residence. Does he know that? Is it part of the reason he chose the location?

Myrrh glances over her shoulder as she creeps toward the opening, noticing that unlike the rusted metal of the grate, the hinges are clean and glistening with oil. The smell of sewage and moss rises from the grate. As she draws within a pace, the expected child detaches from a shadowy corner where a chimney juts from a wall.

"Affiliation?" she asks.

"None." Myrrh glances at the outstretched hand, wondering whether Glint plans to compensate her for tolls.

"Sorry, no entrance." The grubby hand vanishes into a pocket, and the child glances up toward a shuttered window a floor above Myrrh's head. A gesture the girl should have been taught not to use.

"I have no plans inside Maire's Quarter. I only need passage through."

"No grubbers allowed. Go away."

For all the grime worked into her cheeks and the hunched way she carries herself, the girl has sharp eyes. Her gaze keeps flicking to Myrrh's weapon hand. Myrrh glances toward the shadowed corner where the child was hiding. There, a rope—rubbed with soot to blend with the stone—runs up the wall, through a pulley, and into the upstairs window. That's the alarm.

The girl follows her glance, pauses for a moment, then leaps for the rope. Myrrh is faster. She yanks her dagger from the sheath and slams it against the rope, pinning the cord against the stone. The girl yanks on the loose end, but Myrrh presses too hard. She elbows the girl back, careful not to hurt her.

"Run," she hisses, dropping a silver fivepence out of her sleeve pocket and onto the cobbles. "Lay low. Ask for your same job in a couple weeks if you want. They won't remember your face."

The girl yanks harder. Myrrh grabs the rope above and below her blade and holds it tight while she slices.

Then, unfortunately, the child screams.

Sixes.

Myrrh hoped that criminal operations in Lower Fringe had a greater need for discretion than in Rat Town. Seems she was wrong.

She shoulders the girl aside and heaves the grate open. A square of light illuminates the wall on the opposite side of the alley as the window shutter opens. Myrrh jams her dagger into her sheath, drops to her belly on the floor of the alley, and shoves her legs down the hole. She fishes for a ladder rung with her toe as a man shouts for her to stop.

The ladder is slick. Even when she gets toes on the rungs, her feet slip and slide. One rung disappears, too high for her toes. She scrabbles fingers over the cobbles, seeking some kind of grip as her body slides into the hole. Her toes slide off the next rung too. Myrrh throws her arms wide in hopes she won't plummet all the way down.

Her leather sleeves drag over the edge of the hole as she builds up speed. As her palms near the edge, by some whim of the Queen of Nines, the fingers of her right hand catch on a crack between cobblestones. The impact jars her shoulder. She kicks out, landing a foot on a rung, and grabs the uppermost iron bar with her free hand.

The girl stomps on her above-street hand.

"Miser's toes, you're a little imp," Myrrh hisses.

The girl just glares.

Shaking her head, Myrrh yanks her hand from beneath the boot and slaps it on the ladder. As she scrambles down, the girl yells again.

Her boots land on solid ground. A relief, though it wouldn't be the first time she had to wade through sewage. She keeps a hand on the ladder, squinting into the ink ahead. Her eyes water from the stench.

On one side of the tunnel, a narrow walkway offers dry passage beside the stream of sewage. Myrrh takes a first step and yelps when the surface underfoot wobbles. She peers closer and notices gaps between the stones. Farther ahead, wooden planks span longer spaces between stone blocks.

Up above, the first heavy footfalls enter the alley.

Sixes and seeping pox. It's blacker than the Miser's heart up ahead. Back to the wall, Myrrh edges forward and digs into her jacket for the glimmer. Fumbling the packet open, she nearly drops the little ball of resin. Fortunately, it sticks to her finger long enough for her to jam it between her cheek and gum.

The tunnel explodes with light.

With her next breath, cold energy pours into Myrrh's body. She springs forward with icy precision, lands on a stone block a body length distant. Two more long strides bring her to the first plank. Light as a bird, she scampers across the wooden bridge. Looks back. As a heavy boot, scuffed with use, lands on the top ladder rung, she kicks the plank off its blocks and watches it float away on the stream of filthy water.

Whoever controls this access is not going to be happy with her.

She sprints across the next few sections of bridge, kicking each down behind her.

And hopes this tunnel leads to a decent escape.

Chapter Seven

With the glimmer singing in her veins, each drop of condensation on the tunnel walls is a brilliant prism, shattering light into twinkling stars. She steps like a cobra strikes, with lightning quickness and the surety that each foot will find its mark. Behind her, the self-proclaimed owners of the tunnel bumble like oafs through the fetid stream.

With every step, her lead on them grows.

Now she gets why Glint wanted her to have the glimmer resin.

The tunnel doglegs to the right before she gets a view of the exit. A stone wall caps the passage, allowing the sewage out through a low grate in the bottom. Open air lies beyond, the glow of torchlight like a blazing fire. Almost too bright with the glimmer.

Myrrh hurries forward to the grate. The planks she's been dislodging have piled up against the metal, and when she kicks the bars, swinging the grate up on hinges as well oiled as those at the entrance, the boards spill out with a series of splashes as they drop into the River Ost.

Myrrh winces. Not as stealthy as she'd hoped.

She props the grate open with a bar attached to the bottom edge, then crouches, peering out over the water. A wide shadow darkens the river between her vantage and the first support pillar of Fourth Bridge. An island of stone and rubble built to anchor the support slopes down from the pillar's base. Myrrh needs to get over there, but how?

She looks down, scanning the sheer wall beneath the tunnel's exit. Sewage falls over the lip in a wide waterfall. No hand or footholds there.

She looks up. Finds nothing to grab.

This has to be the thieves' route into Maire's Quarter. There was even the expected urchin guarding the entrance, collecting tolls, and barring entry. So what is she missing? Where does the path go? She expected some sort of ladder bolted to the stone, hidden in the shadows of the bridge's great arches. Or maybe a web of rope that an agile thief could scramble up across. Maybe even some sort of zip line with a pulley and handle.

A rope swing?

There's nothing.

She dangles a leg out the low exit, braces an arm on the inner wall, and ducks her whole torso out to feel around. Her hand runs over cold stone while sewage laps at her new leather pants.

Sixes.

She ducks back into the passage. The stench in the tunnel seems much worse after her gulps of fresh air. Thank the Nines, glimmer doesn't sharpen her sense of smell. As she pulls her leg back in, she hears a shout from the river.

Despite her head start, the splashing of some very angry thugs is getting noticeably closer. Myrrh balls her fists. Unless she figures this out, she'll have to choose between facing the oncoming ruffians or taking her chance in the Ost. She's a passable swimmer, but not strong enough to fight the current until she's away from Lower Fringe and the row of guards on the waterfront.

She touches her dagger's hilt, shaking her head. This *shouldn't* be sixing necessary. Why guard the entrance to a dead end?

Another shout from the river as one of the bargemen calls out a rhythm to the men working the poles.

Myrrh stiffens and swipes a hand down her face. *Of course.*

Barge captains use poles to travel near Third and Fourth Bridges because the passages under the bridges are just barely wide enough for the vessels. The *barges* are the thieves' path into Maire's Quarter. And if she'd come here with permission of the syndicate that controlled access, she'd have all the time in the world to wait for a boat to span the gap between the tunnel's exit and the bridge's support pillar.

She shakes her head, disgusted with her predicament. How many gaps between pillars lie between here and Maire's Quarter? How many barges will she have to wait for if she's lucky enough to get across the first gap without her pursuers following? Four? Five?

She doesn't have a sixing chance.

Myrrh sticks her head through the slot. With poles bristling on either side, the barge looks like a long-legged water insect. In the bow, the spotter's lantern flares in the night, sparks leaping off the ripples where the current breaks around the blunt front of the vessel.

The barge won't reach her for at least a minute. She glances back down the tunnel. Light now warms the wall where the tunnel doglegs. The thugs will arrive first.

Gritting her teeth, she draws her dagger. Without the plank bridges, the jump between stone blocks is more than double her height. She takes a breath. Focuses on the glimmer-ice filling her veins. She leaps and lands a foot precisely on a stone block. As the foothold teeters beneath her soft sole, tiny adjustments in the muscles of her lower leg compensate. She jumps again and again, hopping over the fetid water. If she survives this, she can't exactly make her way across Maire's Quarter smelling like she's been wading through sewage.

The lantern comes into view, held high above the shining bald head of a goon three times her size. Hardened-leather armor covers him from neck to boots, and an ugly-looking mace swings in a holster at his hip.

Myrrh yells and sprints forward, feet knifing through the air and lighting for just heartbeats on the stone blocks.

Another rogue shoves into view, not as mountainous as his partner but with a sly look that makes him seem more dangerous. He draws a knife. The steel sings as it leaves the sheath.

Myrrh jumps, kicks off the wall, and redirects her momentum toward the lantern. She knocks the big man's wrist with a solid strike of her forearm. His hand opens, and the lantern tumbles down, spraying lamp oil that catches fire and throws little splatters of flame onto the tunnel walls. As Myrrh shoots out a hand, grabbing on to the man's arm long enough to swing herself back to the nearest stone block, the brown stream swallows the lantern.

The small pools of oil burn blue for a couple heartbeats before winking out. Now she can see, but they can't.

The big man roars in anger, charges for the spot where she landed.

But Myrrh is already gone. Blind in the darkness, the goon crashes into the wall, spraying sewage over the stonework as Myrrh leaps to a platform just behind the sly thief. The man's arms are up in defense. He backs toward her, free hand waving in the air to fend off an approach. She jabs an elbow into his spine.

Even when surprised and stumbling, the man catches his balance and spins, backsteps out of her reach. He rotates his blade in his palm, cocking his ear to listen for her movements.

His partner roars like a bull and charges across the corridor again, arms catching nothing but air.

"Freeze, you idiot," the other hisses. "Actually, no. Go defend the exit."

The big man's brow lowers, a growl rising from deep in his chest. He seems torn over whether to obey. Then, with a glare into the darkness, he turns and stomps for the open grate over the river.

Another shout from the water echoes down the tunnel, this time very close. Myrrh whips her attention to the slot at the end of the tunnel as the nose of the barge comes into view.

She must catch that boat.

With held breath, she jumps forward, once again hopping between blocks. The big man bars the way, his meaty arm too close to the wall for her to leap past. With a shout, she kicks him in the back of the knee. He goes down, hands plunging into the lumpy flow. Myrrh plants a foot on his back, uses it to spring for the exit.

Her glimmer-sight picks color from the bargemen's clothing as they pole the vessel along.

Behind her, flint strikes steel, and another torch flares to life.

Myrrh covers the remaining distance to the exit in two breaths. She dives through the slot, trusting the glimmer and every reflex she gained from Hawk's training. Her hands slam down on the wooden deck of the barge. She tucks her head, turns the dive into a roll, comes up on her feet.

Surprised grunts on either side. The spotter in the front of the barge whirls, mouth wide with shock. Myrrh shakes another silver fivepence from her sleeve, grabs the spotter's free hand, and presses the coin into his palm.

"Please," she whispers, glancing at the barge's cabin. Exposed by a glass-paned window, the captain sits in the glow of a lantern, smoking a pipe and sorting through a stack of papers.

She sprints two steps across the deck and climbs onto a low rail, searching the island of rubble for the best landing spot.

The men on the poles can't stop their work, not with the treacherous water underneath. The pair closest to her stare openly as she crouches, sets her toe, and jumps. She lands smoothly on the jagged pile of moss-slicked stones, slaps hands onto the top of a slanting slab, and scampers up to put her back to the bridge pillar.

Silhouetted by the torch inside the tunnel, the big goon's legs are like trees. Sewage streams around him as he crouches to peer out.

She holds her breath as he waves at one of the men working the poles.

The pole man glances toward the spotter as if searching for direction.

Raising the lantern high, the spotter opens his hand and peers down at the coin. He glances toward the captain's cabin, then shakes his head at the pole man.

The next time the man works his pole free from the river bottom and steps forward along the deck to plant it again, he whacks the thug's outstretched arm. Hard.

Relief floods Myrrh's chest.

By the time the smaller man arrives at the open grate, the barge is out of reach.

He squats, peers out the slot. Fastens his gaze on her. Hatred burns in his eyes.

Myrrh slides around the pillar, back pressed against the cold stone, and takes up position to watch for the next barge to come this way.

It's up to the Queen of Nines to decide whether one will come for her before the goons can cross to her island.

Chapter Eight

The Queen of Nines rolls her a lucky streak. By the time Myrrh reaches the final island, the goons are still two gaps back. But despite her efforts to stay dry in the sewage tunnel, the thugs' splashing covered her with reeking droplets. While waiting for the final barge to bridge the passage between the last island and a storm drain where runoff—not sewage...plumbing in Maire's Quarter carries that *downstream* of their precious waterfront—makes a silvery streak down the retaining wall, Myrrh slips into the Ost, hands clutching tight to chunks of rubble, and allows the water to flow over her head. Far better to enter Maire's Quarter dripping wet than smelling like the inside of a bilge pump.

She holds up another coin when the next barge makes its ponderous way into the gap. At the nose of the boat, the spotter squints as if trying to tell whether she's offering copper or silver. Apparently, he soon realizes that any coin is better than none. He nods and gestures to the deck. She flips him the coin as she boards and is across in three long steps. With feet balanced on the rail, she pries open the grate covering the storm drain. There's no prop bar here, and the grate is heavy, cutting into her shoulder while she kicks free of the barge. Finally, the grate scraping down the back of her leather jacket, she manages to wiggle inside.

She stands and scurries through the tunnel until she finds a ladder leading up and out. Beside the ladder, someone has scratched the sign of the Queen of Nines onto the wall. The universal thieves' symbol.

She swipes water off her clothes and wrings out her hair before climbing into the open air above.

Myrrh slips through Maire's Quarter with her heart in her throat. Even the alleys are so wide the light reaches every corner. She glances back once and sees wet footprints, shining in the glow of streetlamps with leaded glass that fractures the light into intricate patterns. The buildings are tall, taller than Lower Fringe even, and ornate with spires and cornices and gargoyle faces leering down.

She can't hide or skulk or slip through shadows here. If there are thieves' paths in the district, they're invisible to her. At each street corner, she freezes, certain someone will seize her by the elbow, demanding papers or simply accusing her of being a trespasser based on her appearance.

Instead, the worst she earns is a snort of annoyance when someone is forced to step around her. People walk with purpose here. There's no scurrying, no touching of brows or throwing of elbows depending on where one sits in the pecking order.

And after a few blocks of stark terror at moving about so exposed, Myrrh realizes that no one thinks to question her appearance—despite her wet hair and occasionally dripping clothing—because the bridges and waterfront are so well guarded. The denizens of Maire's Quarter just can't believe that a lowlife scoundrel like her could be walking these streets.

Their arrogance makes her invisible.

After making the realization, Myrrh steps into the part like an actor on a platform at Rhemmsfest. She wraps a hand around her blade and walks with a swagger. She's no rogue crossing the district on a contract from a shadowy kingpin over in Lower Fringe. She's a hired guard, private security brought into the Quarter by a merchant with much to protect. While her employer meets with important contacts—maybe even the Maire—she's walking a perimeter. Keeping a sharp eye out for her boss's rivals or, Patron forbid, any seedy characters who might have slipped past the Shield Watch.

By the time she reaches Third Bridge, her worry over finding an escape from the district via a thieves' path is gone. The Shields aren't watching people going *out* of Maire's Quarter. If anything, they're hustling them along to better focus on incoming traffic.

Just to be safe, Myrrh waits near the bridge until a merchant's palanquin approaches. Hidden inside, the merchant won't notice Myrrh sliding up behind, hand on her blade and hard eyes searching the street for any threat to her new "master."

Third Bridge passes beneath her feet as easily as a stretch of muddy street back in the Spills. The moment she's across and out of sight of the waterfront, she ducks into an alley and breaks into a laugh.

The famous Maire's Quarter. Easiest place for a thief to walk openly in the whole sixing city. Who knew?

Her hair has dried, hanks crunchy as she regathers it into a ponytail and ties a leather cord to fasten it. When she probes the vanishing lump of glimmer resin with her tongue, the ball disintegrates into a paste against her gum. Already, her vision begins to dim, shadows once more holding tight to their secrets.

She shrugs. Just one more task to accomplish and she can head back to the safe house.

The long way around this time.

The Neck's night market throngs with people and light. Stalls crowd the streets, a clutter of wood and awnings and sizzling meats. Jugglers throw fiery brands high above the crowd, causing shoppers and wanderers to flinch and scatter. Musicians stand in pools of their own music, whether piping from a flute, drumming, or picking a quick tune from the strings of a lute. Bowls at their feet hold a scattering of coins, often defended by dogs with ragged fur who curl lips at anyone that lingers too long and too close to their masters' earnings.

All manner of wares decorate the tables and glass-topped display cases. Cloth from distant islands. Glittering jewelry. Musical instruments with wood polished to a smooth luster. Plugs of incense send curls of smoke over the market, the pungent trails joining the haze from the cook fires and torchlight.

Myrrh keeps to the bright aisles between stalls, cutting the straightest path she can toward the corner of the market where deals are made on paper rather than by coins exchanged for goods. Fewer buyers wander amongst these trade houses, the structures semi-permanent with real doors and walls offering privacy for brokers and customers.

She scans the placards hanging over the thresholds, ignoring the hard glares of private guards who stand with hands clasped before their belts. There.

Southland Enterprises.

She taps on the door. A shaft of light falls onto the cobblestones when the latch clicks and the door opens a crack.

"Negotiations closed for the night," a woman says through the gap.

A pair of bulky guards with precisely fitting armor edge closer.

"Even under the auspices of the half moon?" She repeats the phrase Glint told her to speak.

She steps back as the door swings wide. A woman with light-brown hair and a jacket ornamented with silk piping nods at the guards who step away. She motions Myrrh inside, then shuts the door behind her.

A brazier burns in the corner of the room, warming the small space. Myrrh edges closer, glad for the heat after her dunking. Her clothes have mostly dried, but the chill remains.

The woman pulls out a leather document wallet and hands it over. Her face is set in distinct displeasure.

"Tell him this cancels our debt. Any further demands will not be answered, and if he does not desist, unpleasant things will happen to whichever"—she curls her lip as she runs eyes down Myrrh's body—"scamp he sends to threaten me next."

Myrrh has been called much worse. She tucks the wallet inside her jacket and leaves without a word. The door clicks shut behind her as she turns for the inland border of the district and the alleys and paths she'll use to make her way back.

***

Glint opens the door before she lays a hand on the latch.

She pulls out the document wallet as she stalks into the dining room. Candles burn warmly in the wall sconces, and though the tablecloth is gone, flames continue to eat away the tapers from dinner, sending wax flowing over the gleaming candlesticks into pools on the table.

"Were you following me?"

"And good evening to you too."

"Well?" She strides to the table and starts picking at the candle wax.

"Early on, yes. I didn't mean for you to see me. Bad timing with the chef dumping his pasta water."

"Why?"

"Why was I following you?"

"Wouldn't it be enough to know whether I came back with your documents?" She drags a finger across the tabletop, noticing a new pair of cushioned chairs against the far wall. Between the chairs, a small table supports a bowl of nuts. Does he always redecorate at night?

"Tonight's work wasn't really about results, though I did need to fetch these papers one way or the other. I'm more interested in my associates' methods than anything. Fleeing down a storm grate with no idea where it leads was an interesting choice. Brazen. I wasn't sure whether you'd survive the pursuit. Porcelain Hand isn't known for mercy—speaking of, that situation with the men who followed you will need resolving."

Myrrh focuses on the flow of air through her nostrils, a slow inhalation, a slow exhalation. "You saw them go after me and didn't help...?"

Glint crosses the room and stands across the table from her. He plants his hands on the gleaming surface and stares. "I didn't think you were the sort of woman who wants to be rescued. You must admit you're an unlikely damsel in distress."

She presses her lips together. When he puts it that way, no, she'd be furious if he'd treated her like a novice pickpocket working her first job.

He nods. "That's what I thought. Anyway, I'm working on securing permission to use the route into Maire's Quarter. In the meantime, best you avoid it. I have other plans for you anyway."

She lays her palms on the table, mirroring his pose. "You assume so much."

"I'm an optimist."

"I need answers before I lift another finger for you. What's in that wallet?" She nods at the folded leather stuck through his belt.

"Confirmation. Bills of lading that prove what Hawk and I feared."

"Which is?"

"It would be best if I start at the beginning. But I need to know...are you in? I can offer you more riches and power than anyone in the city. Eventually, anyway. But I won't give you my secrets without some assurance. Hawk told the truth when he described your abilities—I saw that much tonight. Now I need your word."

She stares at him. Hawk trusted this man—she ignores the pang in her chest at the reminder of how much her mentor hid from her.

Is it stubbornness that makes her want to walk out the front door or something else? Glint represents everything she rejected when she became a freelancer, but she does need a foothold to start over, assuming what he said about Rat Town is true.

"We seem to be at an impasse. You won't tell me your plans without my commitment to join them. But I won't leap into something without knowing where I'll land."

"Hmm. Indeed."

"How about this? I'm not a snitch. And I don't care about syndicate politics. You have no reason to worry about me selling your precious secrets—who would I peddle them to anyway?"

He stands straight, sucks the corner of his lower lip. "I suppose that's good enough for now. Shall we go upstairs? Perhaps you'd like to change out of your work clothes before we speak."

"One more thing: where's Nab?"

He smiles, a gentleness on his face she hasn't seen before. "Sleeping. Practically had to carry him away from the table. He wanted to wait up for you, kept falling forward and knocking his forehead. Would you like to look in on him for proof?"

"I'll trust you. This time."

Chapter Nine

A wardrobe crafted of some dark wood has joined the bed in her room. Burgundy curtains now hang over the shuttered window, and a rug with thick pile lies beside the bed.

"One of my associates hung your spare clothes inside," he says, gesturing toward the wardrobe. "I took the liberty of asking her to fetch you a few more things. If you remain here, rounding out your attire will be up to you."

After he shuts the door, Myrrh swings the wardrobe open. Along with the nicely tailored tunic and trousers from yesterday, there's some sort of long dress thing, which she thinks may be a nightgown—sleeping in the back rooms of taverns and abandoned stilt houses has left her somewhat ignorant of the normal clothing customs. The real surprise is a dress, dark-gray velvet with black slashes. The sight of the gown makes her cringe. It's kind of frightening actually. She snatches down the shirt and pants, noticing two more pairs of boots lined on the wardrobe floor, smooth black leather that laces to the knee.

On one side of the standing wardrobe, there's a column of drawers. She opens the bottom one and finds her old woolens freshly laundered and folded. The next drawer is empty, but her cheeks heat when she opens a third and finds underclothing. Satin with lace accents. He *did* say he had a female associate buy these things, right?

She glances around the room, self-conscious as she disrobes and slides into the underclothes. The fabric is slithery cool against her skin. The softest thing she's ever worn is a muslin jumper. Nothing even close to this. Before she can think too much about it, she yanks on the tunic and trousers. Her hair is still a wreck from the dunking in the river, but the best she can do is pluck apart a few tangles with her fingers.

After buttoning up the sleeves of the tunic, she hangs up her leather work clothes. She hurries out the door before discomfort with all the finery gets the best of her.

Glint waits by the crackling fire in the room where they spoke the night before. He holds a glass filled with a small splash of amber liquid.

"So," he says.

"So," she responds.

"Can I get you a drink?"

She shakes her head as she takes a seat. The warm smell of leather upholstery puffs up around her as the seat cushion exhales.

"Hawk hated not telling you about this, you know," he says, eyes watching the dancing flames. "He wanted to wait until we were more established. More secure. It terrified him to think the opposition might harm you to get to him."

"And who is this opposition?"

He smirks. "Every syndicate in the city. And of course the Maire and the Shield Watch."

"I see. You said you wanted to start at the beginning..."

"That I did. And I suppose the story begins with Hawk. He was the first."

"The first what?"

"My first recruit. Except that isn't quite right. I approached him but never assumed authority over him. We were partners in everything but name; he wouldn't agree to the title since it was me funding the operation."

Myrrh nods. Hawk was always stubborn, and if he didn't put in an equal stake, she has no doubt he would have refused an equal share.

"So you're starting a new syndicate? Is that why you're..." She sweeps a hand around the room. "Is that why I get a feeling you're just moving in here?"

He shakes his head. "I don't think of us as a syndicate. We aren't playing their games. We bear no marks, claim no turf. Our organization doesn't even have a name. I want none of that."

"Then what do you want?"

He rotates in his chair, leans forward with elbows on his knees. Both hands wrap his glass as he fixes her with a stare. "I will own this city. And it will make me and mine filthy, filthy rich."

Myrrh leans back, props an elbow on the chair arm. "That's all, huh?"

He shrugs a single shoulder. "For starters," he says with a wink. "Though I don't want you to think of me as simply greedy. I have reasons for my aspirations. Perhaps someday I'll tell them to you."

She props her chin on her hand as if disinterested in his last comment. He wants her to be curious about him. Myrrh isn't going to fall for the mysterious stranger thing. "So you recruited Hawk when?"

"About a year ago."

"And since?"

"We've grown, one handpicked associate at a time. Ostgard is bursting with tragically misapplied talent. We've watched. When we've identified a particularly adept thief, we've reached out. One by one, we've plucked the gems from the city's criminal organizations. You didn't ask why every syndicate in the city is our enemy, but that's the answer. Most don't yet know why their best thieves and cleverest assassins have disappeared, cutting into earnings and leaving their leaders scrambling to defend crumbling empires. They will though."

"I don't understand where your gigs come from if you don't control turf? Are you like an affiliation of grubbers? Each taking freelance jobs from other syndicates?"

"For now, we exist—no, thrive—in the gaps. We're the net that no one sees, casting wide for the prizes no one else has the guts or the skills to snare. Porcelain Hand might control Lower Fringe and Fourth Bridge access to Maire's Quarter, but they can't field anyone talented enough to pinch the Maire's signet ring from his bedside table."

She raises an eyebrow. "And you can?"

With a wink, he raises his right hand and wiggles his middle finger. A heavy gold band encircles it. Myrrh can't help herself. Her eyes widen as she peers closely at the M worked into the face.

"Speaking of...Maire's Quarter wasn't what I imagined."

He grins. "Never seen a place where thieves can walk openly because the people there can't believe you'd try it? Ironic, isn't it? But for all their conceit, the lax attitude stops on the doorsteps of the manor houses. The merchant cartels are no different than the crime syndicates when it comes to trust. Even if the only people allowed into their ornate foyers and parlors are other traders of their ilk, they staff in-house guards so thick you can hardly walk a hallway without knocking into one."

"So how'd you get the ring?"

"A story for another night, I think. Weren't you concerned about joining up with such rabble as I might lead? Wanted to know what trouble you'd land yourself in?"

Myrrh rolls her eyes. "Fair enough."

"So that was our early plan. Build up resources until we suck the criminal market dry. The weaker syndicates will simply collapse. The others will begin to fight amongst themselves. Meanwhile, everyone who joins up with Hawk and me could plan to see nothing but profit."

"I thought you weren't interested in the petty wars over turf. Isn't undercutting the other syndicates similar?"

"There's a difference. The existing organizations are concerned about *boundaries.* I don't want to battle Porcelain Hand to scratch out a workable area in Lower Fringe. I want to erase them altogether."

"Semantics."

"If you say so." He sets his glass aside with a heavy click and sighs. "That brings me up to now. We were cautious in approaching defectors, and we made our offers so sweet that no one turned us down and went tattling to a boss. But clearly someone fit the puzzle together. Hawk was nervous during the last days. He said he needed to get back to Rat Town to keep an eye on you."

"It was the Scythe that came for him though. Not the Slivers syndicate or Rat Town freelancers. You think someone turned him in as revenge for your meddling in their organization?"

Glint shrugs. "I assume so. But we may never know."

"Sixing pox we won't know. Don't tell me you aren't planning to avenge him."

He chews his lip, anger darkening his face. "I want nothing more. But which is the better revenge: letting our small empire fall apart while I track down his betrayer or utterly destroying every hope that the Rat Town scum will earn a living in this city again? Believe me, the people who threw him to the Scythe will pay."

Myrrh swallows the lump in her throat. "It's hard for me to imagine never finding out why he died. What if it wasn't because you poached talent from Slivers?"

Glint's brow furrows as he considers her words. "I suppose it could be related to our other work. The problem you've helped me with this evening."

"Which is?"

"We recently discovered a situation that threatens the whole enterprise. Threatens criminal activity across the city, in fact."

"Oh?"

"It has to do with the balance of power in the council. Down here in the gutters and alleys, we tend to think of the Maire as our ultimate enemy. Commander of the Shield Watch, ruler of the city council. The nexus of corruption and creator of all our misery."

Myrrh's thoughts flash back to a raid when she was just an urchin groveling on corners for handouts. She remembers the sound of boots as a cadre of Shields marched through Rat Town, roughing up honest workers and throwing her friends into the muck. Again, she hears the sick sound of a cudgel bashing Myck's skull in. The ragman had often flipped coppers to the hungriest kids instead of paying his taxes.

The Maire ordered that purge. He sent criers through the streets afterward to warn Rat Towners about skimping on their taxes. About the evils of vagrancy and the immorality of drunkenness.

She thinks about the yellow light in the streets when she heard the Maire's Scythe had brought half-a-dozen soldiers to carry Hawk away.

Her tongue is thick when she speaks. "He *is* the ultimate enemy."

Glint laces his fingers and drops his chin to them, considering his words. "This is a difficult topic. Yes, he's filth. The worst kind. The city could be burning, and he'd complain if someone took water from his bath to douse the flames." He meets her eyes. "But we need him. And this change in the council threatens to unseat him."

She blinks, trying to fathom what he's saying. "Need him?"

"Have you ever left the city, Myrrh?"

She stammers, still struggling with his previous statement. "I...uh—"

"I don't ask this to condescend. Only to understand what you've seen. You see, before I became...this." He gestures at himself, the loose black tunic open at the throat, soft leather pants, Maire's signet ring glinting on his finger. "I had the opportunity...hmm. The details don't really matter. Suffice to say, I traveled widely, especially among the Port Cities."

Myrrh drags her attention back to the conversation.

"And?"

"And I came to understand how...inept the Maire is at ruling this city. In the ports, especially Ishvar and Tangesh, the streets are pristine. No compost rotting in piles, no rats skittering from the sudden light of a torch. No peddlers dragging carts or beggars hoping for coin."

"So, little room for thieves, you're saying."

"Well, that depends on your perspective. Just because something looks clean from the outside doesn't mean it's not rotten underneath. I wouldn't say there are no criminals. Just that those who haven't fled have been pressed into working *for* the ruling class. Doing all the dirty things the councilmen and trade magnates won't. Mostly, that means enforcing the things most of us turned lawless to avoid. One-time criminals now extort tariffs from honest workers, usually at the tip of a blade. Others eliminate dissent by silencing those who speak up. Permanently."

"You really think that could happen here?"

"I *know* that could happen here. All it takes is a Maire with the will—and the competence—to move street by street. Flushing us out like rats from a fire. And that's the sort of leader who is currently building support within the council. Merchant Emmerst."

"So you and Hawk were planning to undermine this? A pair of crooks with a newborn network of thieves?"

"That's exactly what we were planning to do. It's going to be difficult. Exceedingly difficult. I could really use your help, Myrrh."

This whole conversation makes her feel numb. She stares at her hands. He wants her to support the man responsible for *so much* cruelty...how could she possibly consider it?

"He killed Hawk," she says.

"I know. Set his pet killer on him. The Scythe is the only competent member of Maire's regime. Well, and the underlings she recruits."

"If he's so inept, why does she serve him? Money?"

Glint's gaze wanders to the fire. "That's an interesting tale. Apparently, there's a vow of absolute loyalty between the Scythe's family and the Maire's. Made under the old magic of the crag oaths. The Scythe's father served the Maire when he was just a greedy merchant. Died sometime during the power struggle that led to the Maire claiming his current title. That's when the Scythe took over."

"I still can't believe you want me to help that man *keep* his title."

"Only because the alternative is so, so much worse." Light from the flames dances on Glint's face as he watches them flicker. "It doesn't have to be forever. What we can protect, we can also destroy."

"How do you plan to...keep him in power?"

"The plan is somewhat complicated. But the short answer is I'll play the merchants' game."

"Explain."

"You mentioned earlier that it seems like I'm just moving into this residence." He gestures toward the wall and the ornate furnishings. "Quite true. And from what you've seen, does it strike you as a rogue's den?"

"It's an unlikely place to run your syndicate from."

He fixes her with an even stare. "As I said, I don't think of it as a syndicate."

"Your affiliation of scoundrels and sneaks?"

"Let's call it my consortium of rogues and freebooters."

"Now you're just being difficult."

He winks. "Maybe, but you're less tense when you're distracted by an argument. Relaxation softens those charming features."

She looks away. "It's all just words."

"I suppose I've acquired a taste for verbal sparring after years of negotiations," he says. "I can keep my sharp tongue restrained if you'd rather."

Myrrh leans back and drapes an arm on the chain. "Negotiations, huh? I thought you and Hawk only started this...cabal of connivers and knaves a year ago."

A smile teases his lips. "Well done. I concede to your verbal superiority. And yes, that's true. I was in a different business before this. However, I do believe I've found my calling." He pauses to look about the cozy room with all its finery. "So, as to why I'm just now acquiring enough furniture to make this place livable, I'd like to introduce you to Ostgard's newest merchant, a young man with contracts to sell and eyes on a seat in the city's venerable council."

He stands and brushes his hands down his torso.

"Wait, *you*?"

Glint grins. "Of course. And like any newcomer to the city's trader class, I'm setting up a modest residence here in Lower Fringe. Close to Maire's Quarter and the major markets as well as Third Docks. Away from the tussling for status in East and West Fifth. I'm not here to impress with the cut of my waistcoat or the pedigree of the horses that pull my carriage. I want coin and a voice when it comes to trade policy. And I think I have what it takes to earn them."

Introduction finished, he flops into his chair.

Myrrh tugs on a strand of hair that has escaped her ponytail. "Speaking of, where did you *get* all this lovely furniture, not to mention these contracts you plan on selling?"

"All honestly stolen by my network of pilferers and tricksters, of course."

"I thought you just conceded."

"I'm a sore loser."

She snorts. "So what do you want me to do? And for that matter, why me?"

"Because Hawk claimed you were the most dependable thief he'd ever trained. And that with the proper instruction, you would be the most capable too. I want to teach you."

The intensity in his eyes shows he's telling the truth. But seriously, why? There are dozens and dozens of rogues and cutpurses looking for work in Ostgard. Sometimes, it seems like you can't spit on a Rat Town street without dirtying the shoe of a skulking crook.

"You still haven't answered what sort of job you want me for."

He smiles crookedly, eyes locked on hers. "Some of my ideas are better left for later. But I'll say this. Every merchant aiming for a seat on the city council needs a bodyguard. Someone close. Trustworthy enough to share in all the merchant's secrets. Of course, I can handle my own defense. I need you for the work I *can't* do while wining and dining. They'll never expect that my personal security guard is one of the best thieves in Ostgard."

Chapter Ten

Myrrh wakes without the panic of the morning before, though she's still skeptical of the mountain of goose down atop her body. She swims free, nightgown tangling her legs like weeds in the river. The new curtains slide aside on a brass rod, exposing a real glass windowpane and a view of smoke hanging low over the city, filling streets with tendrils of haze.

It's noon. Maybe later.

She pulls fingers through her tangled hair, clean now after last night's bath in one of the building's many rooms. A scented bath with oils she couldn't identify. Hot water straight from a pipe and a tank on the roof where a fire heats the contents.

She shuffles to the door. Nab is sitting in the hall right outside her room.

He jumps to his feet, relief in his eyes before he pulls a mask over it and changes his boy's excitement into a teen's swagger. Myrrh contains her amusement.

"Nice dress," he says.

"It's a nightgown. I think."

He chews his lip, shuffling, seeming unsure what to say next. So much has happened.

"Oh." He brightens when he remembers a mission. "Glint said to tell you he went out for the afternoon. He'll be back before evening. He said to be ready to accompany him to a dinner."

A dinner? With him posing as a merchant? She needs to wake up before she can consider this information.

"Do you know if there's coffee in the house?"

"Um."

She drops an arm over his narrow shoulders, ignoring his responding stiffness. "Come on. Let's go see."

Downstairs, she pokes her head into the kitchen. The red-cheeked chef, thick around the waist and wearing an apron, jumps when she reaches through the door and knocks on the wall. He's standing over a butcher-block counter flogging some sort of meat with a spiked hammer.

"Madame?" he says.

She blinks and almost laughs at the notion. "Myrrh is fine. Got any coffee?"

His brow furrows, and he hisses toward an out-of-view corner. A boy grumbles and steps forward, hair stacked up like a shock of wheat.

"Well?" the chef says impatiently. "Get the—get Myrrh some coffee."

The boy's nod is sullen, but he shuffles to the far wall, fills a copper pot with water, and sets it on an iron stove.

The chef pulls a bundle of herbs from beneath the counter and starts chopping them with a wicked-looking cleaver. After a moment, he casts a glance her way as if to suggest she move along.

"If you don't mind me asking," Myrrh says, "how long have you worked for Glint?"

"Since he was a wee..." He pauses, seeming to realize he's trafficking in information that might be restricted. "Many years, Madame. Mistress. Myrrh."

"I see. And does he treat you well?"

The man pushes the chopped herbs into a pile. "Tep will bring your coffee when it's finished."

A sideways glance adds to the dismissal. Myrrh steps back and shuts the door.

Nab is lounging at the table, a bare foot up on the polished surface.

"Don't you have better manners than that?" she asks.

"Glint does it."

"Doesn't mean you have to."

"So you're my mother now?" he asks, petulant. But he takes his foot down anyway.

Myrrh takes a seat across from him. Since last night, the chairs have multiplied. A full complement now surrounds the table.

"What do you think of this place, Nab? We can stay. I'm just not sure we should."

He snorts and stares at her, incredulous. Myrrh winces. She hoped he'd at least consider it since she's not sure where else they'll go. Regardless of whether she wants to commit to Glint's criminal enterprise, she's pretty sure he's telling the truth about her prospects in Rat Town. Whoever betrayed Hawk would come for her next.

"You get knocked over the head on last night's job or something?"

Myrrh shrugs. "Did a little swimming in the Ost. Otherwise, nothing so exciting."

"Must just be the bag of rocks you use for a brain then. *Of course* we should stay. When was the last time you got food for nothing? A real bed? Walls thicker than the Maire's underpants...?"

She swallows the argument she was brewing. Thought she was going to have to convince *him.*

"It's not for nothing. The food, I mean. There'll be work."

"You mean like fetching papers from the night market? Like I said, pretty much food for nothing."

"More than that. All this"—she gestures at the multiplying furnishings—"we gotta help earn enough to pay for this kind of stuff. And more. Glint has plans."

He shrugs. "Do I get more of those chocolate tarts? Another bath that smells like flowers? Come on, Myrrh. You really want to go back to sleeping twenty paces from the bog in a shack that will topple into the mud next big flood?"

"I just like to be cautious."

"Glint told me Hawk wanted you here."

A pang at her dead friend's name. Myrrh shoves the sadness down. Can't let it influence her decision. "But Hawk didn't bring me—us—in. Thought it was too dangerous."

"Well, he seems to have messed up that assessment. He sure wasn't hanging out in Lower Fringe when the Scythe came."

"No. And Rat Town isn't an option for us anymore."

"Then stop being such a head-knocked pigeon. This is a good deal, Myrrh."

She glances toward the kitchen and lowers her voice.

"He wants me to be his personal bodyguard, Nab. While he pretends to be a *merchant.* I don't know a thing about security or trader society."

The boy grimaces, then laughs. "What? Miser's balls...*you* protect *him*? Is he crazy?"

"Thanks for the vote of confidence. And don't be vulgar."

"Just make sure he gives me some jobs too. I gotta start stashing loot for when it all comes crashing down."

The kitchen door swings open and the boy, Tep, shoulders out with a china cup and saucer. He spots Nab, then sighs and starts to turn back to fetch a second cup.

"It's okay," Myrrh says. "Nab's too young for coffee anyway. It's not a drink for little kids."

Tep smirks while Nab glares daggers at her.

Myrrh accepts the cup and raises an eyebrow at Nab, daring him to argue like a complaining child. He crosses his arms and puts a foot back on the table.

***

After coffee, Myrrh excuses herself, leaving Nab to sulk at the table. As she steps onto the first stair, she glances back and sees Tep emerging from the kitchen with a set of dice. Was he watching for her to leave? She's long wished for a friend for Nab, the orphan turned urchin turned apprentice thief. Not many kids his age inhabit the Spills, and those who do live there work dawn to dusk at the docks or in Smeltertown.

Nab grunts a greeting, returned in kind by Tep. But after a moment, Nab nudges out a chair with his toe. Tep grins and spills the dice on the tabletop.

That alone is reason for Myrrh to take the job.

She checks the doors on the second-floor landing. Still locked. But on the third floor, near her bedroom, she finds a room packed with crates and shelving. Bottles of wine lie on bolts of fabric that match the curtains in her room. A stack of books teeters in the corner. Drawn to the pile, she runs fingers along the spines. Gold lettering stamped into leather. Titles that speak of faraway lands. Mysterious people. Stories, not the dry histories she learned with.

Myrrh can read. A secret taught to her by Hawk over many long, candlelit evenings.

Did her mentor teach the skill to Glint too?

One of the titles captures her interest. *A Stranger Tide.* What does it mean? To her, the ocean is a distant thing. Mythical. The tides are equally mysterious.

She pulls the book from the stack, straightening the others, and backs from the room. Most of the other rooms on the floor are locked. Except for the pair of double doors opposite the stairwell. She squeezes the latch.

It's Glint's room.

A wide four-poster bed, unmade, presides over the room. Heavy dressers stand beside a small table with a crystal decanter half full of whiskey. There are just one chair and one tumbler.

A bookshelf squats beneath a pair of framed maps. One of the city and one she doesn't recognize but suspects as depicting the Vellos continent and Ostgard's place on it.

Glint can read, it seems. And he's done quite well impersonating the young, rich merchant freshly arrived in the city.

She slips into the room, leaving the door ajar, and pads to a writing desk that sits below the window. The curtains are open. From Glint's room, a sliver of the waterfront is visible, peeking between buildings.

She sets down the book and tries the little desk drawer. Locked.

A stack of papers has been dropped haphazardly on the desk's surface. Myrrh takes a seat and picks them up, begins leafing through. Purchase orders. Shipping receipts. A scrawled note:

Haven second.

Check Ishvar channels for more supply, but use caution over white contamination.

Rumors you may have been recognized in East Fifth.

She puzzles over the words for a moment. Who wrote this? Glint? Hawk? After a moment she shrugs and sets it aside.

The next paper has five columns of numbers and nothing else. No explanation for their meaning. She shuffles it off and peers at the next.

"Finding anything interesting?"

Myrrh jumps to her feet, sending the chair skidding across the floor. Glint is lying on his bed, hands behind his head, long legs outstretched. How long has he been in here?

"I can explain that if you like." He nods at her hands. The paper hangs limp from her fingers.

Myrrh swallows to gather her composure, then sets the paper back on the stack. "I'm guessing you were practicing your sums. You could try counting on your fingers."

"Clever. But no. It's a ledger tracking the price of ores and smelted metals. While considering which goods I—posing as our friend Merchant Giller—would have the most luck trafficking in, I examined the outputs from Smeltertown. It's Ostgard's only industry, you see...all the other wealth in this lovely city is skimmed off the trade in goods that come in and out on the River Ost." He shakes his head. "We're nothing but leeches really. In any case, robbing the ingot trade would do too much harm to Rat Town and everyone that depends on regular shifts at the smelters. I just haven't got around to throwing away that ledger."

"So you're an altruist."

"How do you mean?"

"You won't steal if it harms the poor."

He turns his eyes to the ceiling. "No, just a pragmatist. I need Ostgard to keep functioning or I won't have an empire to rule. And for the city to thrive, it needs shift workers. Who else will shine shoes and empty chamber pots in Maire's Quarter?"

"I see."

"I don't suppose you want to explain why you're searching through my belongings. I was under the impression we were working to establish trust."

"Maybe I didn't know this was your room."

"Maybe you shouldn't lie to the man who wants to make you his closest associate." His eyes remain on the ceiling as if this is a casual conversation, but Myrrh can almost feel the tension in his body.

He's right to be angry at her snooping. But Myrrh can't bring herself to grovel out an apology.

"If you were truly concerned, you should have locked the door."

"It shouldn't have been necessary."

Myrrh sighs. "Fair. I won't enter again without your permission."

"Thank you." He rolls his head to look at her. "Dinner is in two hours. The leathers and your dagger will be fine for tonight, but we'll want to add to your weaponry."

"Where are we going?"

"The merchant's family name is Buliat. We'll arrive together, and I'll leave you posted in front. Once dinner is underway, I need you to find an alternate entrance. Search Merchant Buliat's study for information on his next shipment of Jalla spices. He's something of an upstart, so I doubt he has in-house security. But I can't say for sure."

It sounds easy enough. "Anything else?"

"Feel free to supplement our coffers if you find items that won't immediately be missed."

She nods, looking forward to a simple assignment. "I'll be ready."

"Don't forget your book when you go." He nods toward the desk. "And yes, you can borrow it. *A Stranger Tide* is one of my favorites."

Myrrh feels the blush in her cheeks as she grabs the book, slowly, not snatching.

"Oh, Myrrh?" he says as she steps to the door.

She turns.

"You have my *permission* to enter anytime. Just ask. And that's a nice...nightgown. I think my grandmother wore something similar."

With a glare, Myrrh stalks through the doors and pulls them shut behind her. Hard.

Through the heavy wood, she hears him laughing.

Chapter Eleven

Glint looks like a different man in a buttoned waistcoat over a silk shirt. His hair is slicked back, and the scruff of his beard has been shaved clean.

Myrrh needs a minute to collect herself from the shock. She wouldn't have recognized him if he hadn't come knocking at her bedroom door at the expected time.

He looks her up and down. "Are your boots okay? I was worried they might pinch."

After her swim in the river, the pair she wore last night is still damp. She's laced a pair of the tall black ones over her pants.

"They're fine."

His eyes pause on her dagger. "Tomorrow we start training with the sword. We'll just hope Buliat has little experience with security."

"Would it help if I brought one for show?"

He thinks for a moment. "Better not to be burdened with something you haven't learned to use. I don't anticipate trouble, but we shouldn't be overconfident."

"If there is trouble, can you fight in that clothing?" she asks, casting a skeptical glance at his finery.

He grins and flicks his wrist. Myrrh doesn't even know where the blade in his hand came from, but an instant later, it's at her throat.

"I should be okay," he says.

"I guess so." She feels the embarrassment in her cheeks.

"Though that wasn't really fair. We don't expect our allies to attack. I'm sure you'd surprise me just as easily."

She's not sure, but she's grateful for his kindness in saying so.

"Shall we?" he says. "I have a couple more details to explain on the way."

She checks her weapon and nods. "Ready."

***

Myrrh can't help but feel exposed walking openly along the waterfront. But with Glint leading the way, acting every inch the arrogant merchant, no one pays her any heed. Not even the row of Shields guarding the river.

"I believe I mentioned before, but my family name is Giller," he says as they stroll. "Our major business is in ocean shipping. We have five caravels working out of Tashkal, sailing the main routes to the Hevish Archipelago and Gargoa. My older brother will inherit the business, which leaves me with a minor allowance to found my own venture. I've chosen Ostgard so that I won't be competing against my sibling."

"Does it matter that I haven't heard any of those names before?" she asks.

"You've heard them now, right? Can you repeat what I just said?"

"Family business in Tashkal. Shipping to Hevish Archipelago and Gargoa."

He pauses for her to catch up and grins. "I figured you'd be able to. And as to your question, just by recognizing the names, you probably know more than half the merchants in the city. They're good at pretending but terrible at actually learning something."

"Is that what you go by? Giller?"

"Merchant Giller to most. My close associates may call me Penn."

"Including me?"

"Depends on how close you want to get," he says with a wink. "It can be dangerous to get too familiar with your employer, you know."

"I wasn't asking—"

He laughs. "I know. But it's worth thinking about. The assumption that you and I are having liaisons might work to our favor because people would be more likely to speak freely in front of you. But you'd have to be...convincing."

Myrrh knows she's blushing furiously. Can he see it?

"A strict merchant-and-bodyguard relationship is fine," she says.

Again, Glint laughs. "Fair enough, Rella."

"Rella?"

"Rella Aventile. Does it work for a name? Most personal security comes from merchant-class families who don't have wealth to set up *all* the heirs with their own businesses. Your mother was a wheat baroness from one of the independent territories inland, but the blight from ten years ago wiped out too much of your family's savings."

"Am I going to need to explain all this to anyone?"

"You shouldn't. But always best to have contingencies, right?"

She nods. Fair enough.

Glint resumes walking at a slow saunter, hands in his pockets.

"I will say, though," Myrrh begins, "if Rella were to get into a relationship with the man she's supposed to be guarding, she'd want to be sure he's worth her while."

"Oh?" Glint raises an eyebrow.

"It's a risk, like you said. Could be dangerous for her. But she'd consider it if he shows talent in his chosen pursuits. Speaks to a level of focus that could be attractive to someone like her."

A smile pulls at his lips. "Then perhaps Merchant Giller will feel inspired to show how very well he plays these other traders. He does intend to build an empire, you know."

***

A woman in servant's livery opens the heavy wood door to Merchant Buliat's home. The building is modest by Lower Fringe standards, just two stories, but the intricate ornamentation on the facade and the detached servants' quarters suggest up-and-coming wealth. The residence sits on a low rise, nearly on the border with East Fifth. Glancing at the second-floor balcony that runs along the entire front face of the building, Myrrh imagines the view of the city is quite spectacular.

The balcony is also a likely target for her entrance into Buliat's private rooms.

"The merchant and mistress will be down in a moment," the servant says. "May I invite you in for a drink?"

Glint catches Myrrh's eye to make sure she heard. Don't try to enter until she's certain the Buliats are downstairs and distracted. Myrrh controls the impulse to roll her eyes, remembering that he wouldn't have brought her if he didn't deem her competent.

"Thank you." As Glint steps through the door, he begins to unbutton his waistcoat. Myrrh notices that he doesn't gawk. He scarcely glances at the polished surfaces and glinting chandelier in the foyer. The servant remains in the doorway, and Glint has to take a step back to pass off his coat for her to hang.

"Pardon, Merchant," the woman says as she folds his coat over her arm. "The mistress asked that anyone accompanying you also come inside. Your escort may wait in a chamber we've prepared."

Glint spins on his heels, casually tucking a hand in his pocket. "I prefer my bodyguard remain where she can watch the street. I'm not concerned for my safety in your mistress's lovely home."

"Rightly judged. You certainly needn't be concerned." The servant nods toward an antechamber. A shadow darkens the foyer's floor as a heavily built man in hardened-leather armor steps into the archway. "Rest assured, the exterior of the house is just as secure. We have additional sentries posted nearby. If you didn't notice them on your approach, they're doing their jobs well."

Glint's slow blink is the only sign that the unexpected situation bothers him. He inclines his head politely. "In that case, I'm sure Miss Aventile will be glad to wait in the comfort of your home rather than exposed to the chill night."

He beckons Myrrh forward. With a nod, she mounts the pair of steps leading to the door and steps in, hand resting lightly on her dagger. Not as a threat, but to prove Rella's dedication to her merchant master's safety. She meets Glint's eyes, searching for a hint as to whether he wishes the plan to continue. His shoulders rise in the faintest shrug.

It's up to her.

The home smells of fresh-cut flowers and tung oil that has been worked into the heavy wood furniture. A single bench stands against the marble-tiled wall. As Myrrh approaches the bench, the servant rushes forward and touches her elbow.

Myrrh whirls, eyes narrowed, and the servant gasps.

"Pardon, Miss..."

"Aventile," Myrrh says in a flat tone.

"Miss Aventile. The mistress has prepared the west alcove for you." She scurries forward to an archway opposite the burly guard's antechamber. With a sweeping gesture, she invites Myrrh to enter.

A small table has been set with a flagon of wine and a simple meal of bread, grapes, and cheese. A single chair stands between the table and the alcove's entrance. Myrrh picks it up, carries it to the far side of the table, and plants it where she can sit *without* turning her back to the rest of the home. Leaning over the table, she pulls the food and wine into easy reach.

"Victuals for my hired help," Glint says. "Your mistress is too kind."

The servant bows. "She and the merchant recognize the value of friendships among traders. They hope to forge long and prosperous ties in this city."

"Indeed," Glint says, spinning on his heels. "And how long have you been with them?"

Another sweeping gesture invites him to precede the servant through a grand archway and deeper into the house. "Quite some time. But I won't retain my position if the mistress descends and finds that I haven't offered you the hospitality she requested. Please."

Glint chuckles as he starts for the archway, boots clicking against the polished floor. "I quite understand. My mother was much the same."

Myrrh leans to watch the pair's retreat. A larger room opens beyond the archway, dominated by a grand staircase ending in a pool of gold-toned carpeting. The servant guides Glint to the right of the stairway and through another door into what Myrrh assumes is the dining room.

Across the foyer, the guard grunts and steps back into the alcove. He takes a seat in a straight-backed chair and turns his attention to the front door.

Myrrh plucks a grape off the vine and pops it into her mouth. This isn't going to be easy.

Chapter Twelve

Myrrh eats enough to make her appreciation of the hospitality believable; most guards would be relieved to earn a night's pay without working for it. In the time it takes her to finish the meal, the guard gets up once, stomps to the back of the foyer, and disappears behind a screen. The sound of liquid splashing into a pot eliminates her idea of asking to use the bathroom and quickly slipping off to find those sixing papers Glint wants.

After maybe half an hour, Merchant and Mistress Buliat descend the stairs. The woman's gown swishes with each step, dragging on the floor. Her hair is pinned atop her head in a ridiculous arrangement that looks like a gob of horse apples. The merchant, in contrast, wears simple linen trousers and a loose-cut shirt belted at the waist.

She takes his arm as they alight on the gold carpet, and he leans close to whisper something before they turn for the dining room.

Mistress Buliat glances over her shoulder, and Myrrh looks away just in time.

When they vanish from sight, Myrrh yawns and stretches. She scoots back from the table and exits the alcove, swinging her arms as if to limber them.

"Nice gig here," she comments as she strolls toward the guard's alcove.

He grunts as she leans a shoulder against the support for the arched entry.

"I'd been looking for a good, consistent employer for a while before I found this. Worked barges between here and Glendarn before Merchant Giller made his offer."

Up close, she notices his eyes are a touch red. Glassy. Maybe he was out drinking too late last night. She also catches him glancing at her dagger. Alone, it *is* a strange choice of weapon for a bodyguard. The reach is too short. But at least she's small, which makes it slightly more believable. Still, she should have at least two blades close at hand. Or better, a crossbow for range.

He sticks a thick finger in his ear and scratches. "Worked a few vessels myself. Back before I landed in Ostgard. Tough work."

"Least it stays interesting, right? Not so much sitting and staring at doors."

She's not sure if the low sound in his throat is a laugh or a growl. Hopefully a laugh. His eyes linger on her breasts, and she waits for his disgusting suggestion on what they could do to make the time pass.

The leering does give her another chance to think about those bloodshot eyes though. *Something* kept him from getting a good rest last night.

"So, got any dice?" she asks.

His callused fingertips fidget with creases in his heavy canvas pants. Leaning out of the room, he flicks a nervous glance toward the rest of the house. So, it *is* gambling that keeps him up late.

"Can't," he says, obvious reluctance in his voice.

Myrrh huffs and waves off his concern. "I've been with Merchant Giller for half a year. Started providing security for his negotiations all the way down in the Port Cities. These dinners take hours."

He glances toward the dining room again. Shakes his head.

"There are two of us. More than enough to protect this hallway, right?"

"My dice are in my quarters. I'd have to go out and get them."

Myrrh's eyes widen ever so slightly as she remembers the detached servants' quarters behind the house. She'd hoped to distract him with dice while she thought of something else. But this is even better. A boon from Lady Nine.

"No problem. I'll watch the door for you."

He glances at her dagger as if skeptical.

You don't expect a strike from an ally. Remembering Glint's earlier actions, she springs. In half a breath, her blade is drawn and against his throat. The guard bats it away easily and raises a fist. She backs away, laughing and raising hands in surrender.

"No harm meant. How about this...I'll give you double odds on the first round. Nines and threes both."

It's almost a sure bet that he'll clean out whatever purse she brought with those odds. The man's internal battle is obvious on his face. His willpower loses.

"Lock the door. Knock is three taps, pause, then one. No one else allowed in."

"Three then one. Got it. No one will know you were gone."

With a grunt, he stands and lumbers toward the exit. A wash of night air swirls into the room when he opens the door. Myrrh rushes forward the moment he pulls it shut. She twists the deadbolt and dashes for the archway leading to the rest of the house.

From the dining room, she hears the clink of cutlery and the low murmur of voices. Occasionally, the mistress of the house titters, but the discussion is otherwise between Glint and the other man. By the sound of it, the conversation is amiable if not downright friendly.

Now where is the study?

A smaller exit leaves the grand hall opposite the dining room. Unlike the wide archway, this is sealed by a closed door. Upstairs, a railing encircles the hall, providing a view down from all angles. At least half-a-dozen rooms open off the balcony. Other than the double doors, which she assumes lead to the bedchamber, the study could be behind any of them. She doesn't have much time, so she'll have to hope she gets lucky. Starting with that downstairs room.

As she slips into the grand hall, she spots the servant. The woman was nearly hidden on the other side of the stairwell's stone banister. She's standing with arms clasped behind her back and an attentive eye on the dinner proceedings.

Sixes.

Myrrh had hoped the woman would double as a kitchen servant, ferrying courses and empty plates to and from the kitchen.

But she doubts she'll get another chance. The guard won't take long to fetch something from his quarters.

She creeps, heel to toe, along the wall toward the downstairs door. Every few paces, low tables stand against the wall, displaying vases and statuettes; Myrrh is exceedingly careful to give them a wide berth.

One step after another, she approaches the door.

A loud laugh from the dining room makes her jump. She whips her head just in time to see the servant turning her attention back to the room. Inside, Myrrh can now see the table, easily as long as Glint's but set for just three.

Glint takes his hand off his belly as he recovers from his overly enthusiastic burst of laughter. He dabs at his eyes as if wiping away tears, and as he lowers his napkin, his eyes meet hers, flick to the servant, then return to hers with an intense stare.

The message: he just saved her from being spotted.

She nods in gratitude, then hurries on. Can't worry about mistakes that didn't happen.

Unfortunately, the door is locked.

She thinks of the lockpicks she tucked into a pocket in her sleeve. No. Not enough time. Especially when she doesn't know whether it's even the right room.

Swallowing, she turns to face the stairway. She still has time to get up there and search a room or two.

But it means passing within a pace or two of the servant. No matter how stealthy she is, it's too risky.

Unless Glint can help.

Sliding away from the door, she catches his eye again. Because of the table's orientation, he's the only person with a direct view of the main hall. She points to the stairs.

His brow furrows as he looks at Merchant Buliat. After listening to something the man says, he gives an exaggerated nod.

Was that meant for her?

Myrrh's got no idea, but either she gives up now, or she hopes Glint has a plan. She creeps forward and lays a hand on the stair railing.

"Excuse me," Glint calls, motioning for the servant. "Could I trouble you for a white wine?"

Mistress Buliat instantly starts patting the carafes they've already supplied, clearly horrified that her guest needed to make a request.

Glint puts on the sort of smile Myrrh didn't even know he had. A complete heart melter. He sets a calming hand on the mistress's wrist. "It's just that I get phlegm, you see. It comes from my coastal ancestry. White vintages are least likely to cause me distress."

Myrrh contains a laugh and crouches down as the mistress motions furiously for the servant. Moments later, she's up the stairs and on the balcony, hurrying for the first door. A closet.

A grin spreads across her face when the second door leads to her target. The massive desk and heavy wood shelving leave no question that she's found the right place. She runs forward and starts rifling through papers.

Fortunately, Merchant Buliat doesn't keep nearly the number of stray papers Glint does. Just a quick search turns up a shipping manifest for Jalla spices that shows the cargo left Ishvar a couple weeks ago. Myrrh has no idea what that means for arrival here, but it will have to do. She quickly straightens the papers and dashes out, shutting the door quietly.

She dashes for the stairs and then stops short.

The servant is back, but now she's pacing back and forth in front of the stairs.

Chapter Thirteen

Sixes on top of sixes.

There's no way she's getting down the stairs. And she's pretty sure Glint's done what he can unless he wants to throw this whole dinner down the storm grate.

Can't go down, which means the only option is out. Which also means she needs another way back *in*, seeing as she barred the sixing front door. But *that* problem is going to have to wait.

Thinking of the second-floor balcony she noticed from the street, she focuses on the door nearest the front wall of the house. But that's no good, because didn't Merchant Buliat mention sentries? She'd be pretty sixing noticeable climbing down right over the street.

The back wall of the building is going to be the best bet. Which means going through the merchant's bedroom.

With her shoulder skimming the wall, Myrrh slips toward the double doors. They're right at the top of the stairs. In plain view of the servant's pacing.

Myrrh needs to be smoke. So smooth she can hide in plain sight.

She creeps forward, each motion as slick as glass. The doors stand just ahead.

Down below, the pacing footsteps continue. She can't look, can't tear her focus from the door latch. Her hand reaches forward. Cool metal slides under her palm. She squeezes the latch and feels resistance followed by a click.

Footsteps continue, back and forth. No hesitation. Just impatience and annoyance that the dinner is taking so long.

Myrrh breathes in through her nose, out through her mouth. Nudges the door open.

It glides on silent hinges. The temptation to leap forward is almost irresistible, but Myrrh slides slowly through the gap. Risks a glance toward the stairs as she turns to guide the door shut.

She can't hear the footsteps anymore. Can't see over the edge of the top step. She makes the sign of the Queen of Nines and hopes as she presses the door closed. Slowly, she releases the latch.

A single candle burns on the nightstand beside one of the twin beds. The flame dances in the breeze from the cracked-open window.

Above a dresser, a set of hooks holds necklaces. Gems and gold and glass beads glint in the candle's glow. So many. Myrrh hesitates half a breath before running over and snatching a gold chain with a thumbnail-sized jade pendant surrounded by twinkling emeralds.

If she's bungled tonight's task so badly that it's the last job she does for Glint, at least she'll have something to help fund a relocation.

She hurries for the window, tucking the necklace into a jacket pocket.

The drop is about three times her height. Taller than she thought when looking up at that balcony. Grimacing, she wrenches the window open, earning a groan from the frame, and lowers herself out, feetfirst.

Even dangling by her fingertips, her toes are a good ten feet above the cobblestones of the alley. Good thing she knows how to roll.

Myrrh lets go, braces, hits hard. First her ankles, then knees, then hips wrench with the strain. Her back hits the cobblestones, and she rolls, her spine crunching over the uneven rock.

She coughs as she stands, wincing. Her right ankle isn't right, aches deeply. Hopefully it's just a sprain.

Fifty paces away, a door opens. The hulking guard from the foyer steps out, shaking a pouch of dice. His head is turned the other way, toward the alley exit.

Myrrh sprints and leaps onto his back. With a low yell, she yanks out her dagger, flips it hilt first, and clubs him in the temple. The man crumples, taking her down with him. His bulk slams onto her already-injured ankle. She bites down, holding tight to a scream, and presses against his body with her other foot until she can get her pinned leg free.

He groans but remains unconscious.

Myrrh stands, squeezing her forehead between her thumb and middle finger, gritting her teeth against the pain in her ankle. Sheathing her dagger, she darts into his quarters and searches until she spots a bottle of cheap liquor. She yanks out the cork and rushes outside, grimaces as she grabs his stubbly chin to pull his mouth open. She pours out more than half the bottle, some of which goes down his throat. The rest splashes over his face and neck.

He sputters and coughs, rolls over, and falls still.

Quickly, she sets the bottle outside his door, grabs the dice pouch, and throws it under the cot inside the room. Finally, she searches his pockets, curling her lip at the feel of his body heat, until her fingers brush a metal key ring.

Thank the Nines.

Thinking of the sentries the merchant claimed he'd stationed outside, she does a quick scan of the alley. But if someone were watching, they'd be on her by now. Especially since she just dropped out of their master's bedchamber window.

She gives the man another knock on the head for good measure. He needs to stay unconscious for a while. She feels a quick, guilty pang, but then she remembers his leering gaze and bloodshot eyes. Serves him right for staring at her breasts like that.

Myrrh runs to the end of the alley and peers out. Clouds scud over a half moon, painting shifting shadows across the stone walls and streets. A light fog gathers near the ground, slowly swirling. From here, the street falls away toward the river, streetlamps standing like sentries in pools of their own light. Long streaks of torchlight reflect off the River Ost, wavering in the current.

She takes a breath, then slips forward, scanning the scene for sentries with every step. Still, no one challenges her.

At the building's front corner, Myrrh waits until a thicker band of clouds slips over the moon, then hurries forward and fumbles through the set of three keys until she finds the one that fits.

She sighs in relief as she twists the latch and steps inside.

Three faces greet her arrival. Glint's hard gaze pierces her, while the merchant and mistress simply stare in openmouthed shock.

"Mistress, Merchant," she says, curtsying. "You're finished with the meal already?"

"What's going on?" the mistress finally manages to say. "Where's Gendall?"

Glint is a granite statue. Myrrh's thoughts race as she approaches the Buliats, offering out the keys.

"I didn't wish to spoil your evening, especially after you've offered such hospitality." Myrrh pauses until Merchant Buliat raises a hand, a perplexed expression on his face, and accepts the key ring. "Shortly after you started dining, your guard said he needed to patrol the perimeter."

Mistress Buliat lays a hand on her husband's arm. "Did you give him that instruction? I asked him to keep an eye on"—her eyes flit to Myrrh—"to watch the front door."

"Well, as far as I can tell, he was more interested in keeping an eye on a bottle of liquor. When he hadn't returned by the time I finished eating, I wondered if something had gone wrong. I needed to know for the sake of my master's safety. No offense intended. I noticed that...Gendall did you say? I noticed he'd left his keys, so I locked the door behind me so as not to leave you undefended while I went searching for the problem."

"And?" Mistress Buliat says, voice ever so slightly shrill.

"It appears the issue was with his taste for alcohol. I'm sorry to say I found him passed out behind the building."

Merchant Buliat's face purples with anger. He stalks to the door.

"Merchant Giller," he says, "I'm horribly ashamed over this. I hope it doesn't detract from the fortuitous discussions we've had tonight."

"Not at all, Merchant Buliat. I know quite well how difficult it is to find loyal help, which is why I feel so lucky to have found Miss Aventile."

“Then if you’ll forgive me, I have a situation to deal with. Perhaps we can meet again in the near future.” The merchant opens the door, but Glint doesn’t move.

“Merchant Giller?” the mistress asks.

“Quite sorry, I’m merely looking around for my coat.”

Once again, the mistress is horror-struck by the lapse in her hospitality. Her face goes so red Myrrh wonders if it actually hurts.

“Clea! The merchant’s coat! Now!”

Merchant Buliat shakes his head. “If she hadn’t alerted us to the guard’s absence, I would consider letting Clea go due to this inattention. Accept my apology, again.”

“There’s no need, my new friend.” Glint turns on that smile again, and even Myrrh finds herself a little wobbly. The servant comes racing out, apron askew, and shakes the wrinkles from Glint’s coat as she hands it out.

“Terribly sorry, Merchant,” she says, touching her brow.

“Think nothing of it. Much like your master, I am grateful for your attentiveness in the other situation. And for your generosity in filling my wine tonight.” He winks as he tugs the waistcoat over his shoulders.

“Until next time?” Merchant Buliat asks as he extends a hand.

Glint clasps it firmly. “Until then.”

***

“Aren’t you worried about the sentries?” Myrrh hisses once they’ve put a couple blocks between them and the Buliat residence. She managed to hide her limp while in sight of the building, but now it’s crept into her gait.

Glint looks over his shoulder as if also calculating earshot from the merchant's. He raises a finger as they cover another block.

At the next corner, he grabs her hand, pulls her toward the edge of the street. He releases her and puts his back to the wall.

The laugh that comes from his belly is so genuine she can't help smiling.

"That," he says, tipping his head back against the wall as he unbuttons his waistcoat, "was the most fun I've had in months."

"Fun?"

"Yes, fun." He tugs her arm, urging her to join him, backs to the wall. "Look around."

"At what?"

"The night. The shadows. They're ours."

Myrrh scans the street, but the darkened alcoves and alleyways seem more menacing than enticing right now.

"I guess I'm still on edge."

"Makes sense, I suppose. You did have the hard job this time. Maybe next time I'll take it a bit easier on you, eh?" He nudges her with an elbow.

Myrrh blinks, still feeling out of sorts. "You didn't know they'd invite me inside."

"No. But still. You did well. We'll plan better in the future to avoid unnecessary risk. As for your question about the sentries, there were none."

"How do you know?"

"One, I would have seen them. That's not arrogance. It's just one of my strengths. Two, Buliat wouldn't have cared about keeping you inside and under guard if he had men outside watching your movements. None of the merchant class trust each other. They see people like us as crooks and liars, but they're the real scoundrels, no sense of loyalty to anything but money. As soon as they spy weakness, they fall on each other like starving dogs."

He pushes off the wall, turns, and rubs his hair to destroy the slicked-back look. It falls almost into his eyes, banishing the high-society gentleman and restoring the unrepentant rake. "So...?"

"So, what?"

"Did you get the information?"

She snorts. "Do you think I went to all that trouble to fail?"

His teeth shine in the moonlight when he grins. "Excellent."

"I grabbed this too." She pulls out the necklace, forgetting her plan to hold on to it as insurance for leaving his operation.

He gives a low whistle. "Nice. I'll introduce you to a fence tomorrow."

"You don't want it?"

"You earned it. All I did was sit around and drink wine." His brow furrows. "Tell me how you hurt your ankle."

"You noticed?"

He goes down on one knee, ignoring the fact that the dirty cobblestones will ruin his trousers, and lifts her injured leg onto his other thigh. He presses a hand against the top of her foot. "Can you pull back against pressure?"

"So you're a healer now too?"

The joking expression is gone from his face when he looks up. "No, but I learn what I can to take care of my people. Can you pull?"

She winces as a sharp pain travels up her leg when she tries to press her foot harder into his hand. He nods, then presses against the side of her foot, again asking her to resist the force. The examination continues for a few minutes, and then he gently places her boot back on the ground.

"A sprain, I think. Lace the boot tight for a couple days, and you should be good."

"I was worried I broke it."

"I figured." He stands and brushes off his pant leg. "I know you'd protest if I offered to carry you home, but what do you say to me lending a shoulder?"

Slowly, as if approaching a startled horse, he steps up beside her and slips a questioning hand around her waist.

Myrrh considers objecting until she tries to weight the foot and pain shoots up to her knee.

"Fine."

"So," he says as they start off, her arm over his shoulders for support, "what did Rella think of Merchant Giller's performance tonight? Is he up to her standards?"

"Ask her after she has a nice warm bath and a glass of his best whiskey."

Chapter Fourteen

Glint is away for much of the next few days. Myrrh's happy to lie in bed, injured foot propped on a pillow, reading *A Stranger Tide*. The book is about a pirate queen who carves out a territory in a chain of islands Myrrh hasn't heard of. For all she knows, they aren't even real.

On the fifth or sixth day after the adventures at Buliat's, she's completely wrapped up in the story—a monstrous sea creature is attacking the queen's fleet—when a knock comes at her door.

"Yeah?"

She expects Tep with another tray of food. He's brought three since she woke, enough she feels a bit like a stuffed sausage.

Instead, a stranger's face appears as the door swings open. A moment later, she spots Glint with his hand on the door latch. Myrrh tugs the covers up toward her chin and narrows her eyes.

"You see," Glint says to the other man. "Even my sister's a reader. It's just my little rat of a brother who's been so stubborn."

His sister?

The man clears his throat, clearly uncomfortable at seeing her in bed. As well he should be. Myrrh shoots Glint a glare.

"And now your *sister* would like her privacy restored, thank you."

Glint responds with an amused smile. "As you wish, dear sibling."

As soon as the door clicks shut, Myrrh jumps out of bed, wincing when she accidentally steps too hard on the ankle. She hops to the wardrobe, drags off the nightgown, and pulls on her linen clothes. Her ankle is swollen like an apple, but she shoves it into one of the boots and cinches the laces tight. Grits her teeth and tightens them more.

Out in the hall, she hears voices coming from a room two doors down.

"I don't care about reading!" Nab sounds like a whining five-year-old.

Glint backs out of the doorway, chuckling. "In this case, Harold, I'm afraid it doesn't matter. Father has tasked me with furthering your education while you're fostered here."

He spies Myrrh and tosses her a wink.

"This is so stupid!"

"Young man, I'm afraid it's critical that someone of your pedigree know how to conduct written business," the tutor says in a calm voice. "Your brother has informed me of your previous difficulties, and I assure you we'll work through them. I see you have a writing desk here already. Shall we begin?"

Glint watches for a moment more before latching the door. He turns a grin to Myrrh. She's not sure what to say. Without Hawk, she figured Nab would never have the chance to learn.

He must see the gratitude on her face because he shrugs. "Needed to keep him busy with something, right? Can't have a half-trained thief rattling around my house looking for ways to amuse himself."

It's a poor excuse. Myrrh lets him use it though.

"Are you heading downstairs?" He offers an arm, which she refuses, preferring to limp. He's done enough for her today.

"I can't lay around *all* day."

He shrugs. "As far as I'm concerned, what good is roguery without a healthy measure of indolence? Anyway, I met with some of our associates this afternoon. The leaders. I informed them about what you learned at Buliat's."

"You met here?"

He shakes his head. "It would destroy my reputation to have a bunch of miscreants and thugs knocking at the door."

"Hmm. So the rest of your organization remains a mystery. I've begun to think I'm the only person you've convinced to join up."

"Well, there are the men I sent to abduct you."

"Right. Aside from them I suppose."

He takes the stairs slowly, keeping pace with her limping gait. "Do you have a plan, or are you just walking to delay your healing?"

"I thought you were going to help me fence my pickings from the mansion."

"Ah," he says. "Well, if you insist. Perhaps we could visit a tavern while we're out."

***

The fence, a man with gold teeth and beady eyes, cocks an eyebrow at her. He stands behind a battered wooden counter, thick fingers inspecting the jade-and-emerald pendant. "Not going go be easy for me to sell."

Myrrh narrows her gaze, scanning the room. A low ceiling presses down over their heads, the rafters dark with soot from a fireplace that crackles along one wall. Judging by the smoke spilling out the top of the fire chamber, the flue doesn't work very well.

Glint steps forward and leans an elbow on the counter. No doubt ready to step in on the negotiations. Myrrh lays her palms flat and glances at him. She doesn't need help.

"I suppose I'll find someone more talented then."

The fence turns yellow-stained eyes her way. "It's a unique piece; that's the problem."

"Fortunately, Ostgard is the center of trade for an entire continent. Even if there weren't a thousand merchant families in the city alone, all with more money than they can spend, there are traders from as far away as the Hevish Archipelago."

Out of the corner of her eye, she spies Glint's smile at her use of the name she learned just a few days ago.

The man shakes his head and sets down the necklace. "So you say, but I've been in the business for a long time. Takes caution not to attract the wrong interest. I assume the previous owner would not be pleased to see her necklace on the market."

Myrrh sighs and plucks up the chain, flipping the pendant into her hand. The man's eyes widen slightly, betraying his surprise.

"A shame." She turns to leave, poking at the pendant.

"Wait," the man says quickly. "I didn't say I wouldn't sell it."

"Quite true. But you see, after being forced to argue, I came to a realization. Such a large city..." She opens the catch and clasps the necklace around her throat. "I don't actually *need* the funds right now, and what are the chances the former owner frequents the same establishments as I?"

She pushes the door, which despite its rickety appearance—no doubt crafted to give the impression of poverty—takes measurable force to open.

She glances back as she steps into the dim light of the alley. Glint is still standing by the counter, shaking his head in bewilderment. After a moment, he dashes forward. She shuts the door behind him.

"What are you doing?" he asks.

"Just as I said. I've decided I quite like the necklace."

"He was only negotiating. It's expected. But he fetches some of the best prices in the city. Jak handles most of my business…it's hard to find a good fence."

"And after tonight, I imagine he'll think twice about trying to swindle you or your associates in the future."

Glint sighs as he steps into the evening light slanting onto the main street. Passersby step around him as he looks at the sky in exasperation. Myrrh joins him, ignoring his beleaguered act. Finally, he sighs and tucks hands into his pockets. Playing the part of a merchant out for a casual evening, he wears a loose leather jacket over a silk shirt. It suits him better than the waistcoat but not quite so well, in her opinion, as proper thief's garb.

He glances at her, meeting her eyes before sliding his gaze down to the pendant. With gentle fingers, he straightens the stone so that it lies flat against her breastbone just below the hollow of her throat.

He cocks his head and smiles crookedly. "It does suit you."

She snorts. "No more than that gown thing your associate bought for me." She thinks of the strange velvet garment still hanging in her wardrobe.

"I mean it, Myrrh. It's nice."

She blinks, unused to compliments of this sort.

He smirks. "So, ready for that drink?"

***

Myrrh and Glint sit at a corner table in an establishment that's nothing like a Rat Town tavern. At high tables scattered around the room, men and women speak in low voices and sip colorful drinks. Not one insult is thrown across the barroom floor, a space of dark wood planks without a hint of sawdust scattered to collect vomit and spilled drinks. The only musician is a woman in a long red gown who plucks a slow tune from a harp.

Do these people actually enjoy such a sedate atmosphere?

The barmaid approaches, clad in a straight black skirt that ends well below her knees and a bodice that shows only a hint of cleavage. Her eyes linger on Glint as she steps up to the table.

"What will it be?" she asks, finally managing to drag her eyes to Myrrh.

"I don't know. Ale, I guess."

The barmaid's brow furrows, and Glint lays fingers on Myrrh's wrist. "Let me buy you a Tendun whiskey." He turns a sneer toward the barmaid. "You do have that variety, don't you?"

"I have—yes, sir. We should have one bottle."

"Please see that the portions are generous."

As the barmaid scurries off, Myrrh curls her lip. "What's wrong with ale?"

"If you ask me, not a thing. But this is Lower Fringe. These people have to do *something* to pretend at the sort of snobbery that will gain them audiences in the Fifths. Even if that's eschewing a perfectly good beverage."

Myrrh snorts. "I'd like to see them try drinking in Rat Town."

Glint grins, leans back, and drapes an arm over an empty chair. “Indeed.”

The drinks arrive, deeply hued liquor that smells faintly of smoke and burns a line down her throat and into her stomach. Myrrh sips twice, then sets her tumbler down and cups a hand loosely around it. She watches these pretenders at high society while they strut and posture.

No, she doubts this is fun for them. But for her, it makes for pleasant entertainment.

“So, I have a couple things to discuss that make this more than a social evening,” Glint says.

“Oh?”

“As I mentioned, I met with my leadership today.”

“And?”

“Buliat is a strong supporter of Emmerst, the merchant at the heart of the plot to unseat the Maire.”

“You didn’t mention that before.”

“I wasn’t certain until we spoke at length, but Buliat managed to hint at the Maire’s inadequacy multiple times.”

“So do you plan to use him to get to Emmerst and the council?”

Glint shakes his head. “Not enough influence. But I can keep him from throwing too much support to the plot. Or rather, you can.”

“What do you mean?”

“I mentioned I had plans for your future involvement in the organization.”

“You really ought to give it a name. ‘The organization’ just doesn’t have much of a ring.”

He smiles crookedly. “Maybe *you* ought to give it a name if it will shut you up.”

He nudges her leg under the table, making sure she knows he's teasing.

"So what are these ideas?"

"All this information gathering and working from the shadows becomes tiresome, don't you think? It's time for a good old-fashioned heist."

"Hmm. What do you have in mind?"

"The spice shipment. I'll give you four men. Good, solid thieves who follow orders without question."

"You want me to lead it?"

He nods. "The shipment is due at Third Docks before dawn three mornings from now. We'll apprehend it before it makes port."

"How much of the shipment?"

"Every crate aboard the barge will do nicely," he says with a grin.

She sips some more whiskey as a slow smile stretches her lips.

***

"And what will Merchant Giller be doing while I'm stealing the contents of a barge?" she asks as they stroll home along the waterfront. A cold fog has settled over the city, its chill pressing through her thin clothing. Her ankle aches ferociously, but she gets the feeling it would be even worse if not blunted by the whiskey.

He sucks his lip while thinking. "You know merchants. Giller will probably be over in Maire's Quarter hoping to be *seen* in some of the fine eateries and drinking establishments."

"You have the papers to cross Fourth Bridge?"

He raises his hand, wiggling his finger. The Maire's signet ring has been spun so that the crest hides in his palm, but he's still wearing it openly.

"I didn't pinch it just for fun," he says. "The papers are simple to forge. The only difficult part is the seal. Easy if you have his crest to press into the wax though."

"I see. And the good Merchant Giller isn't afraid to move about Maire's Quarter without protection?"

His pace slows, and he glances at her sideways. "Is Rella that concerned to let him out of her sight? Maybe she's decided to consider a relationship after all."

She rolls her eyes and keeps walking before he can notice the blush on her cheeks. At the next intersection, they turn. The front door of Glint's residence is straight ahead. As she approaches the door, he touches her shoulder, making her jump.

"All teasing aside, I'm safe in Maire's Quarter. But you'll be moving through the lower half of the city to intercept that barge. Keep your head up and your face down. We still don't have answers on Hawk."

She looks away. When Hawk died, she vowed to get vengeance. And she's done *nothing* to find his betrayers. After this heist, she will find a way to dig deeper.

"Hey," Glint says as he steps close. "We *will* get revenge for his death. And we'll make sure to honor his legacy by building the empire he envisioned."

She shrugs, not ready to meet his eyes. "He deserved better."

"I know." He lays hands on her shoulders.

Myrrh pulls away and turns for the door. "I have a heist to plan."

Chapter Fifteen

Myrrh's eyes sting from the smell of river water. Upstream, maybe a half hour's walk, First Bridge is a line of floating torches above the Ost. Downstream, the river swirls and stinks until the braided channels that drain the western bog inject water that merely smells of algae and stagnation. It hasn't rained in a few days; that's the real problem. A good downpour would flush the contaminants from the Smeltertown slag heaps rather than leaving them to trickle in. Plus it would blast the sewers clear for a while. In any case, Myrrh's eyes start to tear as she walks onto a rickety pier that juts from the muddy bank. The flimsy wood wobbles in the shifting currents as she squints and searches downriver.

Buliat's shipping manifest, carried here by a pigeon, according to Glint, has the barge arriving in the wee hours tonight. At least, that's what Glint calculated. Myrrh is skeptical that the vessel will appear on schedule. But Glint was adamant. It has something to do with shipping permits and congestion around the Ostgard bridges. Captains that miss their dates pay hefty fines on top of the tariffs the Maire charges for passage and trade.

Somewhere on the riverbank behind her a bird warbles. The breeze is blowing downstream. Occasionally, it carries a bit of laughter or a shout, sounds of the usual debauchery in Rat Town and the Spills. Near where the pier joins the bank, Les, one of the thieves assigned to her, and incidentally, the man she kicked in the gut on the night of her abduction, sits in a waiting rowboat. The oars knock against wood when he reaches for his waterskin. The cork comes out with a pop, and she hears faint noises from his throat as he drinks.

Otherwise, aside from the splash of the river against the pier's posts, the night is still.

There. Exactly when Glint predicted.

Myrrh smirks, glad she didn't make a bet against his calculation. The barge cuts upriver, too silent to hear from here, but surely pulled by the splash of oars. A lantern floats above the vessel's nose, held aloft on a spotter's pole. Shadow still cloaks the vessel and crew, but not for long.

She pulls out a small whistle and trills off a series of notes that sound like birdsong. A few hundred paces downstream, three more rowboats detach from the riverbanks. Oars muffled by cloth wound around the paddles tug against the Ost's stinking waters. Already, the thieves aboard will have dosed themselves with glimmer. To her men, the barge will appear as clear as if it's advancing upriver under a noonday sun.

Down below, Les looks up expectantly, waiting for her command. His eyes begin to gleam silver as the resin takes hold, but Myrrh's hesitating. She wants to give her other senses a chance to read the situation. The sounds from the barge. The breeze raised by the river currents. They'll disappear under the glare from the glimmer-sight.

"Not yet," she says softly. "I have a better view here."

He nods and checks the stowage of his small rucksack and waterskin. Raises the oars in readiness but doesn't shove off the bank.

The swiftest of Myrrh's little vessels skims across the river toward the lonely light at the front of the barge. Slowly, more details of the vessel emerge. She spots the angular lines of the cabin and the faint glint of moonlight off the river-wet oars. Moments later, the rowboat disappears behind the bigger vessel. Myrrh makes the sign of the Queen of Nines.

No alarm goes up. The barge's oars continue their rhythmic churning. Myrrh's rowboat appears on the far side of the barge, the thief inside raising a single oar to indicate success.

No unnecessary harm to innocents. That was Myrrh's goal, along with a successful operation. The three thieves on the water carry small crossbows armed with darts dipped in nightbark serum. The raised paddle means the man at the barge's tiller, likely the captain of the vessel, has been darted.

Quickly, the thief reverses course and rows into the barge's wake where he'll board from the stern. Meanwhile, the other two rowboats move in.

Myrrh finally pulls out her ball of glimmer resin and tucks it into her cheek.

The world explodes with light as her men fire darts into the necks of the pair of guards standing amidships with eyes on the water. The guards sway, teeter, and fall bonelessly to the deck. It takes a few breaths for the oarsmen to understand their protection has abruptly disappeared. Then the first shouts go up. Night air carries words as if they were spoken in her ear.

"Treachery!"

"Pirates!"

The last brings a grin to her face. She's hardly the pirate queen from *A Stranger Tide*, but this is a start.

"Now," she says, waving Les forward. He stabs a paddle into the mud and shoves back, bringing the rowboat directly beneath her. With the glimmer, she lands lightly in the bottom of the boat. Though the little vessel wobbles as Les begins to row for the barge, Myrrh stands as easily as if she's on level ground.

Aboard the barge, the lantern goes flying as the spotter whirls. The lamp turns end over end. A pool of fire spills across the deck. Immediately, the thief already aboard whips off his cloak and starts beating at the flames. Her men still on the water dodge the strikes of oars and row for the back of the vessel where they quickly leap aboard.

Swords come out, throwing wild glints in her glimmer-sight. The moment her thieves draw their steel, at least half the oars hit the decks as their bargemen surrender. The others brandish paddles like they're pikes.

The barge starts to yaw, turning broadsides to the current. Myrrh gasps and steps to the front of her quickly approaching rowboat as the barge's deck rocks when the river grabs hold.

"Cease!" Myrrh yells before blowing a shrill note on the whistle. Responding to the urgency in her voice, Les rows faster. They knife through the water toward the vessel. On deck, her men easily bat away thrusts from the oarsman. But she needs to get the big boat righted. Finally, they draw even with the barge, easing up near the stern.

"Dart one of the oarsmen," Myrrh shouts as she snatches the anchor rope from her rowboat and executes a perfectly aimed leap to land on the barge's deck. She loops the rope over the same bollard where the other rowboats have tied up. With a few running steps, she jumps and catches hold of the roof of the cabin. Her feet paddle against the wall as she vaults up atop it. The deck is in chaos. The only good news is that the fire is out now, thanks to the quick work of her man.

As she steps to the front edge of the roof, a dart streaks from the rowboat and sticks in an oarsman's neck. He sways, then topples. The other bargemen's eyes go white rimmed.

"Anyone else?" she shouts.

The oarsmen drop their paddles.

"Good! As you may have guessed, we are apprehending this vessel. Anyone who doesn't accept that can get off with your fellow crew." She nods to the thief who is inspecting his cloak for holes burned into the leather.

"On it," he says. He grabs an unconscious guard by the feet and starts dragging him toward the stern.

Myrrh glances at the shore. The barge has drifted farther downriver than she hoped.

"No one? Okay. Then if you want to live, I suggest you get back on those paddles."

Men jump to obey.

Another of her thieves hurries to take the tiller as the bite of the oars slowly brings the vessel around. The barge begins to surge forward as coordinated paddling pulls it upriver.

"All right," she shouts. "Now, seeing as I'm a forgiving person, I'm prepared to offer you more than a chance to survive the night. This barge is about to become property of my organization. We'll need men to work the decks. Prove your worth tonight, and I'll consider keeping you on."

She glances toward the nose of the ship where the spotter crouches, trembling. "But not you," she says, nodding at him. "You set fire to your own vessel."

He jumps up, hands clutched in front of his chest. "I—I don't want to die, missus. It was a mistake. Just—I'll serve you well, I swear!"

She laughs. "Shoot him."

His face screws up as Les aims another dart. The man shrieks when the point plunges into his neck. As he slumps to the deck, a couple of the bargemen moan in fear.

Myrrh jumps down, landing gracefully with one foot on a spice crate.

"Oh, stand straight, you cowards. They're not dead, though they may have headaches when they finally wash ashore." She gestures toward the stern where her men are loading the first guard into a rowboat. One thief stands in the bottom of the small vessel, taking the man's feet under the seat so he won't fall out if he startles awake. Her man hands up the oars before climbing out and casting the little rowboat free.

The bobbing vessel is soon lost in the darkness, sure to carry its passenger well past dawn before someone spots the helpless boat and fishes him out.

Her men repeat the process, loading a man per boat while she watches the shore for the main channel where the bog empties into the river. With the distance they were swept downriver, she's sure they'll need to paddle back to reach it.

"Hew closer to the bank, if you will." She squints. There...the glimmer-heightened flash of starlight off water looks promising. She climbs onto a crate near the rail, hoping for a better view.

Myrrh scarcely has time to turn when the cabin door flies open, cracking against the outer wall. A young man sprints out, hair tousled with sleep. He charges toward her as she slaps for her dagger. Myrrh jumps backward, trying to escape his wild punches. Suddenly, he freezes. She spots the dart stuck just below his hairline as one of her thieves dashes forward and delivers a kick to the boy's ribs. His eyes open wide with shock as he topples, the side of his knee catching on the rail and tipping him headfirst into the Ost.

"No!" Myrrh runs for rail, just in time to see a paddle crack against the boy's head.

He's limp now, facedown, the nightbark in full effect.

Myrrh's rowboats are gone. The water's not fit for swimming here; the flux gained by swallowing just a few drops often kills.

No doubt, the boy has already inhaled the foulness, probably swallowed it too. There's nothing she can do for him.

She watches his body recede on the current, just another bit of flotsam. A hard stone fills her throat as she clenches the low rail in a white-knuckled grip.

Behind her, silence reigns over the vessel.

"I would appreciate it if no one else tries any foolish heroics," she says, forcing herself to stand straight. The bargemen still need to continue to fear her. With every ounce of will she possesses, she steps again onto a crate and regains command.

She points to the channel where they'll leave the Ost. It's deep enough for a ship to weave away and out of sight from the Ost, but only if the helmsman knows the way.

Which Myrrh's does.

Feeling anything but the pirate queen she imagined herself less than an hour ago, she stands near the prow of her new prize as they row it to safety.

***

Carp's Refuge is as much a haven for misfits and hermits as it is a stopover for smugglers using the bog to bring goods around Ostgard. Members of both groups watch from weathered boardwalks and ramshackle shanties as the barge cuts through the morning sunlight on its slow passage into the settlement. Quite a few residents choose the occasion of their passing to start sharpening blades and oiling crossbow mechanisms.

Myrrh stands in the nose of the barge, scanning the houseboats and hovels for signs leading to the Frog's Whistle pub. She's never been to Carp's Refuge before and has sometimes wondered whether it was just a rumor. Not much smuggling work for a grubber from Rat Town. Ordinarily, the chance to see something new would have her alert and grinning. Not to mention, the successful capture of a whole sixing barge. But she can't stop seeing the shocked look on the young man's face as he toppled overboard.

She didn't kill him, exactly, but it's the closest she's ever come.

The settlement is organized around a network of channels, much like streets in an ordinary town. But here, nothing is so permanent. The denizens of Carp's Refuge move as the flow of water and attention from the Shield Watch fluctuate. She's heard stories of smugglers rowing into Ostgard for a night of carousing in the Spills only to find the whole Refuge vanished when they returned at dawn.

Along with every bit of loot the smuggler was bringing through, of course.

That won't happen to her score. At least two people will stay with the barge until it's emptied, cleaned, and refitted so that no trace of its previous owner remains.

She shakes her head. A whole sixing barge. Scant weeks ago, she never would have imagined.

Finally, she spots the Frog's Whistle, marked not by a placard hanging outside, but rather by the row of drunks sleeping on the boardwalk outside the front door.

They tie up directly in front of the semiconscious patrons who grumble and roll over, pulling cloaks over their heads to shut out the morning sun.

Myrrh debarks and pushes through the flimsy door into the darkened interior. The glimmer's been gone for more than an hour, leaving her tired and clumsy, not to mention half blind in the dark. She clenches her jaw to keep her focus as she searches the nearly deserted establishment for Jak, the fence.

He smiles insincerely when she spots him. Sitting at the far edge of the bar, he's bent over a cup of coffee.

"Where's your necklace?" he asks.

"Wouldn't you like to know?"

He smirks. "Ahh, Myrrh. Perhaps we got started wrong. I'd like to offer a gesture of peace if you're willing. You're rather more...talented than I first assumed."

"You mean you thought I was a petty thief bringing you the results of my best night's work, and now you're getting a notion of my capabilities?"

"Something like that. Coffee?" He waves for the bartender, a gray-faced man who looks unready to be awake.

She shakes her head. "Just water."

When the bartender pours, little bits of sediment sift to the bottom of the glass. Myrrh shoves it gently away. "On second thought, have any ale?"

The bartender snorts and taps her a foaming mug.

"Like I said," Jak says, "I apologize for our first introduction. Seems you brought in quite a haul." He leans to glance out the open door.

"No more than I planned to take. Glint told you the arrangement?"

"I fence half the spices now, and he stores the rest to put on the market at a rate that won't be suspicious. He didn't suggest anything for the barge though."

"No, that wasn't strictly part of my mission. I just found it easier to take the whole thing than find a place to unload. I've planned a refitting. After that, I'm not sure. Have to talk to Glint. Or maybe I'll just keep it as my share of the haul."

"Indeed?"

"Indeed."

"Well in that case, maybe I can look forward to fencing the fine goods you smuggle on it."

"Perhaps."

Les steps through the door and takes a seat beside her.

"Found a raft that can take you to the Spills."

"What did the bargemen say about staying on?" she asks. She left him to negotiate with them, figuring the use of an intermediary would impress upon them her authority.

He smirks. "I think they're far too scared of you to say no."

"Good. Offer room and board in Carp's Refuge while the barge is refitted, plus extra for any who wish to help with that work. I'll take a small sample of our pickings and head into the city. Glint will send others to help with the unloading."

"As you say...Mistress."

Jak raises an eyebrow. "Mistress, huh? Never met a woman kingpin. What's that make you, queenpin?"

"Just find us some buyers for that spice," she says, downing half her mug in a few long pulls. "I'm going home to bed."

***

Myrrh drops a coin into the raftman's outstretched palm, hikes the satchel full of spices onto her shoulder, and steps onto the muddy streets of the Spills. The raftman's pole makes a sucking sound as he plunges it into the muck to shove off again. Myrrh pulls her hood up over her hair and starts forward.

She's thinking of Glint's warning about the lower districts and what happened to Hawk. But by the time she crosses out of the forest of stilt houses in the Spills and into the crowded buildings of Rat Town, she realizes there was no need to worry. It's still well before noon. Far too early for the lowlifes of Rat Town to be awake, much less on the hunt for a grubber who disappeared weeks ago.

As she winds through the familiar streets, her exhaustion and regret for what happened with the young man start to bleed into her memories of Hawk. She spies a tavern where they used to drink and listen to stories about heists gone wrong and near misses with the Shields. The porch out front is filthy with an overturned spittoon, dust, and spilled drinks. But it was home once, just like the rest of this sixing district. As she stares at the darkened doorway, her lip starts trembling. She wants so badly to go inside and smash things until someone gives her answers.

Hawk was betrayed here, likely by someone he called a friend. Things just shouldn't happen that way.

But it's not the time for revenge. Glint is right about that. Someday, she'll turn this filthy town inside out. But not this morning and not armed with only a dagger and a satchel of spices.

She turns away from the tavern door and trudges on.

At First Bridge, crows and pigeons pluck at crumbs where the once weekly Rat Town Market must have sprung up last night. The stalls are gone now, the pickpockets vanished into their holes, the sellers of mystery meat counting their coins and moving on before someone with a sick child comes knocking. She shuffles over the bridge, legs leaden. Beyond the yards where dockworkers and a few buyers trudge between warehouses, the chimneys of Smeltertown already belch black smoke. Myrrh sways, struck by exhaustion as she thinks of the long walk between here and Lower Fringe.

Eyelids sagging, she sighs and heads for the waterfront where a handful of carts and horses wait to taxi merchants and buyers.

The cart driver she approaches scans her leather thief's garb and asks for half his payment up front. She hands it over gladly, slumps into the cart seat, and dozes most of the way to Lower Fringe.

The man wakes her with an unkind jab from his crop. Myrrh rolls her eyes but hands over the rest of her payment before stepping down. The last two blocks to reach Glint's home seem to take forever, but she finally knocks on the door and shoves it open.

Glint jumps up from the table where he's breakfasting on a steaming heap of eggs.

“You’re back! I figured you’d stay in Carp’s Refuge—is everything okay, Myrrh?”

“We took the barge and everything on it.” She sags against the wall as she pushes the door shut. “A boy died.”

“Sixes.” He’s at her side in a heartbeat, slipping one arm around her back and another behind her knees. He lifts her easily, pulls her against his loose-fitting shirt.

She shakes her head. “I can walk…”

“Oh, just be quiet. Let me help.” He carries her across the room and up the stairs, breathing lightly with the effort. At the door to her room, he crouches to get a hand on the latch but doesn’t set her down. Only once he’s reached her bedside does he stoop to lay her gently on top of the covers.

She swallows and tries to sit, but he waves her off and circles to the foot of the bed to unlace her boots. One by one, he tugs them off, then slips her legs gently beneath the covers.

His thumb brushes her cheek, wiping away the single tear.

“Rest now. We can talk later.”

Myrrh falls deeply and instantly into a black sleep.

Chapter Sixteen

Sometime while she slept, she wiggled out of her leathers and kicked them into a heap against the wall. Myrrh doesn't remember. But when Glint opens the door, carrying a clinking backpack, he blushes and immediately retreats.

Myrrh looks down to see the slinky underclothing keeping her decent. Barely.

She drags the covers to her chin. "You can come now."

Glint clears his throat as he enters. The glow of candles, not sunlight, illuminates the corridor. She must have slept through the day.

He sits on the edge of her bed and starts digging through the backpack. Myrrh's not in the mood for curiosity, so she stares at the ceiling.

"Buliat's piping mad. Roaring at the Shield Watch and dockmasters. Accusing them of losing his barge."

She drops her arm over her forehead. "The captain will wash up eventually to tell the tale."

"But he doesn't know where you took the ship."

"No."

"Hey, Myrrh?" He pauses. She still doesn't look at him. "Can I tell you a story?"

"Can it wait?" The sight of the boy's shocked eyes stabs into her thoughts again. She dreamed about him.

"Hmm." He abandons the backpack for a moment and shifts. "Look at me."

She flicks her gaze his way, then back to the ceiling.

"A real look."

"I'm not in the mood."

Quick, showing the thief reflexes he often hides, he pounces so that his hands are on the covers to either side of her shoulders. His face hovers above hers, hair falling on either side. She rolls her eyes but finally meets his. It's too much work to avoid his gaze.

"It's not your fault, what happened with the boy."

"It was my operation. I should have checked the cabin."

"Accidents happen. Most people attempting a heist of the level you pulled off wouldn't bother to spare lives."

"That doesn't make it okay. The kid's still dead."

"Let me ask you this. If you knew he was the one who killed Hawk, would you feel differently?"

Myrrh struggles against his weight on the comforter. After a moment's hesitation, he lets her sit up.

"*Was* he involved?" she asks.

Glint shakes his head. She wants to slap him for that instant of hope.

"Then why did you say that?"

"Because I want you to listen to my story."

Now that she's sitting, comforter around her body like a cloak, she has a view of the backpack he brought.

"Don't you think I earned a day to get over what I did first?" she spits, gesturing at the collection of swords and throwing knives in the canvas bag.

"Actually, no. I think you'll want to learn what I aim to teach you today."

"How to kill in new and interesting ways?"

"How to disable an opponent without causing fatal wounds."

"Oh."

He raises a hand as if to brush strands of hair from her face but then drops it. "When I was fifteen, I watched my mother beaten to death by thugs hired by a particular consortium of merchants."

She blinks. "I'm so sorry."

"Me too. I would have killed every one of them if I'd had the training and strength. I attacked, but they batted me away as easily as if they were swatting a fly. A single man was able to restrain me, no matter how I fought. And I had no choice but to watch."

"That's why you asked about Hawk."

He nods. "Because I believe you'd take a life without regret if it meant protecting someone you love."

"The boy wasn't hurting anyone."

"You're right. And I am so sorry you have to face what happened. But you can't let it take you out of the fight. My dirty little secret is that I don't just want to rule this city for the power and wealth it will bring. I want to make the merchant filth beg for mercy. I want the people who betrayed Hawk to regret what they did every minute of their pathetic lives."

"After your mother...is that when you became a thief?"

He fixes her with a considering look. "I'll tell you the whole story someday. But it's a longer tale than we have time for tonight."

Myrrh nods. "Fair enough."

With a deep inhalation, he turns his attention back to his sack of weapons. "So, are you up for some practice?"

"I should probably get dressed first."

A mischievous smile touches his lips. "But it would be so much more *interesting* to see you fight in that...attire."

"Go." She shoves his arm.

He raises his hands in mock surrender as he stands and then picks up the sack. "I'll see you downstairs."

***

"Like this." Glint's breath tickles her ear as he steps in and grabs her wrist. He squeezes and twists with just the right pressure, and the sword falls from her grip, clattering to the floor. Another hand snakes around her lower back as she tries to back away. He rotates his hips, drops to a knee, and somehow bends her backward over his thigh. She bucks her hips, trying to spin around and slip free, but ends up with one wrist pinned to the floor, the other trapped between their rib cages.

His face hovers inches from hers. Glint's dark eyes seem to pin her as easily as his weight does. He's out of breath, despite the ease with which he took her down. Easing a knee to either side of her thighs, he releases her wrist and pushes up to hands and knees.

Myrrh swallows. Okay, so *that* wasn't what she expected out of this training session.

"Somewhere in there, you want to constrict blood flow to their neck to cause them to pass out," he says, eyes still locked to hers.

"Miser's little toe, you two are gross."

They both stiffen at the sound of Nab's voice. The stupid little flea has just entered the dining room, an obnoxious swagger in his step and a thin reading primer in his hand.

"We're practicing swordplay," Myrrh stammers as she climbs to her feet.

"Uh-huh. And tell me, is Glint good with his sword?"

Myrrh blushes furiously as she glances at the pack of throwing knives. If she puts one through Nab's sleeve, will it shut the kid up?

"Mistress Myrrh hasn't had the chance to experience my full talents," Glint says easily. "Though I think we've just established that her defenses against them are weak."

Miser's flaccid coin purse. Her cheeks are so hot Myrrh has to stalk to the window and peer out to get herself under control. Full dark cloaks the city, tendrils of mist hovering near grates and potholes.

After a few deep breaths, she turns. Glint and Nab burst out laughing.

"Worthless rats," she mutters.

"So how's the reading going?" Glint asks.

Nab responds with a glare.

"That fun, huh? Well, keep at it." Glint chuckles and turns to Myrrh. "Had enough practice for a while? I have a few things I'd like to discuss with you."

"Given the way she's breathing, I think she could use a lot more *practice*," Nab says.

"I went by our old squat early this morning," she snaps. "Still unoccupied. Maybe you'd like to *practice* relocating."

He grins and sticks out his tongue. "Naw. From what I've seen, you're sorely in need of a chaperone."

Myrrh rolls her eyes. "Can we talk upstairs? I really don't want to have to look at Nab's face any longer than I have to."

Glint finishes tucking the weapons back in the sack before standing and slinging it over his shoulder. "We wouldn't want to interrupt his *studying*."

Nab groans as they head for the stairs. At the second-floor landing, Glint stops and unlocks the door. Tosses the sack inside.

"What's in there?" she asks.

"Mountains of loot. Piles of gold coin."

"Really?"

"No just the stuff I don't want guests to see. Or rather, the stuff Merchant Giller can't be seen with. Some of which is loot from our previous operations, but mostly it's weapons and such."

He shuts the door firmly and relocks it before heading up. As he ascends, she can't help noticing the change in his gait. Straight shoulders, lifted chin, no glances to take in the surroundings. Almost as if the mention of his role as a merchant brings out his arrogance. He's good at shifting personas. Better than she could be anyway.

Inside the sitting room, he flops into a chair. Over the past few days, she's noticed that Tep keeps the fire banked and the supply of whiskey and wine stocked. The red-faced chef, whose name she hasn't learned, seems responsible for the cooking and maybe a bit of cleaning up. Just two servants scarcely seems enough to maintain a merchant's home, but they somehow manage. No doubt Glint needs to be careful who he brings into his employ.

"I've had some discussions with my leadership over the past days. Wine?"

"I just woke up."

He winks. "And after the sound whooping you just received, you wouldn't want to let your guard down against someone of my skills."

This time she refuses the bait. "Now that I know your tricks, you won't find it so easy."

"Then you'll have a glass?"

"Fine."

He stands and runs fingers over the bottles on a side table before selecting one with a purplish hue. The goblet he hands her is warm from the heat of the fire.

"Anyway, it seems I've been falling short in my duties."

"How so?"

"Our organization has grown. Almost fifty strong now. When Hawk was alive, I could count on him to keep things running while I pretended at being a merchant. I can't just step out of a dinner to deal with a pressing issue. So my leaders have been left hanging when they needed direction."

"So nominate one to make decisions when you can't."

"That's the thing." He swirls his wine. "I picked each of them for a specific talent. None have the ability—or frankly, the integrity—for me to feel confident giving them free rein over the direction we take."

"Can you find someone else?"

He stares at her. "I think I already have."

"Wait, what?" Myrrh smooths the legs of her trousers.

"You never gave me an answer. Are you up for leaving the freelancer life behind for good? I can't promise you'll be as free as you were as a Rat Town grubber, but I *will* keep you from being bored. Running the day-to-day operations of a criminal organization is a challenging task. I'll do my best to teach you before the time comes, but I won't be able to think for you when it arrives."

She stares at the fire for a long while before casting him a sideways glance. "No."

He blinks, totally dumbfounded. "Really?"

"Not unless you consider letting me give this band of villains a proper name."

He laughs and taps his toe. "Hmm. I'd have to think about that. But perhaps we could start with a title for you."

"Leader of crooks and lowlifes?"

"How about Mistress of Thieves?"

Chapter Seventeen

A few days later, Myrrh finally manages to drag herself out of bed before noon. Proud of herself, she pushes the curtains open and squints against the bright late-morning sun. A couple days ago, Glint presented her with a few more sets of clothing, winking as he mentioned something about the custom of doing occasional laundry in polite society. If the garb wasn't so sixing comfortable, she might have punched him for that.

She slips on the first outfit that her hand falls on, a loose tunic and trousers of sky-blue silk. Totally impractical for anything but lounging around a pretend merchant's mansion, but she has no other plans for the day.

Tucking her book under her arm, she heads out to find something to drink and a comfortable chair. Tep casts her a long-suffering look when she pokes her head into the kitchen, but produces a cup of warm coffee that wafts a delicious aroma to her nose while she climbs the stairs to the sitting room.

Unfortunately, Nab is enjoying the fire.

Well, not enjoying.

He's clutching fistfuls of hair in his hands, growling at the large lettering in his latest reading primer.

Myrrh takes careful steps back, using her best thief's stealth to avoid his attention.

"Glint wants you," Nab says as she turns for the stairs. "And I don't mean in *that* way. This time."

She shoots him a glare, but he doesn't look up from his book.

"And where am I supposed to find him?"

"Sixes if I know. His room?"

She sighs and leaves Nab to his struggles, tiptoeing back down to the third floor.

"Come in," Glint calls when she knocks.

He's at his desk, looking at the contents of a small silver bowl. She doesn't miss the smooth motion when he slides the desk drawer shut. The lock engages with a click.

It shouldn't bother her. Everyone deserves their privacy. But still.

"Your spice haul has made us temporarily rich," he says, pinching a group of gems from the bowl and letting them fall one by one. "I owe you a night on the town."

"A thieves' carousing, or sedate dinner and drinks as Merchant Giller and Rella?"

He stretches his legs out, crosses them at the ankle, then puts his hands behind his head. "*That* is an interesting question. So many facets and considerations...but the celebration will have to wait. I need to introduce you to the leadership. No matter the circumstances, they won't take your promotion easily, but they won't take it at all if you're a stranger."

"I thought you were going to wait to put me in charge. There was something about teaching me what the sixing pox I'm doing?"

He stands and crosses to the table, dragging his desk chair. "Sit. You shouldn't have to drink your coffee standing up. And yes, I want to wait. But it depends on how events unfold. My senior associates are already agitated because I haven't been able to give the...acquisitions arm of our operation the proper attention. Been too focused on the political side of things. I can leave them to grumble for a while, but eventually, I'll face a mutiny if I do nothing."

She takes a seat and sets the saucer down, bringing the coffee cup to her nose for a deep breath. "So you'll finally show me the central hideout for the 'Organization Glint Refuses to Name'?"

"Eventually. But not tonight. I've invited them here for dinner."

"I thought you couldn't be seen hosting a rabble of miscreants."

He smirks. "Which is precisely why they're going to have a chance to practice their manners."

"Oh?"

"Formal attire, arrival at dusk. If anyone tries to pick a pocket on the way here, they're out." He draws his finger across his neck.

"That's harsh."

"I'm kidding. Sort of. But Merchant Giller will need to start entertaining guests eventually. Might as well have a bit of a dry run."

She looks at him over the rim of her cup. "So I take it you'll be needing Rella's services tonight?"

He raises an interested brow. "As much as Merchant Giller might appreciate the...attention. No. Tonight the same rules apply to you as the others. I seem to recall Lavi hanging a gown in your wardrobe."

The smile falls from her face. "Seriously?"

"Quite. I'm looking forward to the entertainment of watching you try to walk in it."

She sighs.

"But on an *actual* serious note, this is important, Myrrh. I don't want to pressure you, but you need to make an impression on them. They know you have some skills. Word got around about the spice theft. But it will take more than that to make them want to follow you."

"I take it falling down the stairs in a ball gown isn't the impression you're hoping for."

He rolls his eyes. "Just be yourself. Except for the part where you act like an upstart grubber from Rat Town."

"Thanks for the encouragement."

"Anytime." He winks.

Chapter Eighteen

Myrrh isn't sure how to fasten the gown. It has buttons up the back, which no matter how she contorts, she simply can't reach. Who came up with this idiotic garment design?

She tries slipping out of the sleeves and spinning the dress around to fasten the buttons. But then the sixing thing won't slide over her breasts despite the slickness of her satin underthings.

Finally, she undoes the little row of ebony-wood buttons, drags the stupid thing on properly, and slips out the door of her room. The air in the hallway cools her poorly defended back as she peers through doors trying to figure out where Nab is hiding.

"Struggles, dear?" Glint asks, a smile in his voice.

"What possesses women to wear something like this?" she asks, whirling on him.

He shrugs and leans a shoulder against the wall outside his door. He's wearing a tailored coat over a white shirt with loose laces over his chest. The cartilage in his neck bobs as he meets her eyes. "Honestly? I don't know. If you want my cynical guess, it's because somewhere along the line, a man got involved in the design process. He wanted to control your ability to clothe yourself, as monstrous a notion as that seems. Though I admit it looks nice on you. Can I help?"

Myrrh stomps over barefoot and holds her hair out of the way, presenting her back. Deft fingers pull the fabric tight and slip the buttons into place.

"There," he says, low voice close to her ear. "Tomorrow, remind me to have Lavi show you the way to our tailor. Once I make my move into trader society, we'll have to entertain, and I'd hate to have to dress you every time."

She steps forward, away from his breath on her shoulder.

"*We'll* entertain? I was under the impression you wanted me to manage the organization so you could separate your criminal activity from your playacting at being a merchant."

He pushes off the wall and steps up beside her, offering his arm. "That's the beauty of the situation. When it was Hawk who planned to take over operations, keeping him out of sight would have been advisable. No trader with half a wit would believe Hawk was an upstanding citizen. But I'm certain you can pull it off. They'll be too busy looking down your bodice to notice the dagger in your hand. As it were."

Myrrh hesitates for a moment before sliding her hand into the crook of his elbow. Under her fingers, his bicep tenses and relaxes as he tucks his hand into the fold of his jacket. He stops at her door.

"What?" she asks.

"Most people wear shoes to dinner."

Myrrh whips her hand away. "Don't wait. I'll see you down there."

He smirks. "If you insist."

***

Myrrh hears the guests before she reaches the second-floor landing. Raucous laughter. The clink of glasses. She counts three bawdy comments as she descends the last flight of stairs.

It sounds like a Rat Town tavern in the dining room, but the view inside the room is everything Rat Town is not.

A new chandelier hangs from the ceiling, blazing with dozens of candles. Silver gleams on the table, cutlery and pitchers polished to perfection. Rugs have been spread across the floor, not the deep pile of the sitting room, but rather the intricate weave of Ishvar artisans. Each one had to have cost more than she made in the last *year* of nightly freelance gigs. She hasn't a clue how the organization will pull off enough heists to present Glint as a man who slaps down half-a-dozen carpets like this in just his dining room.

She stops at the entrance to the room, taking the measure of the guests.

There are seven. Dressed in finery easily as ornate as her velvet gown, but also dripping with gold and jewels, not one looks like a thief. Myrrh might as well have walked into a dinner at the Maire's palace. Except for the banter and the wine stains already decorating the tablecloth.

Standing at the head of the table, Glint calls something to Nab, who is seated halfway down the table. The boy lifts a glass and grins adoringly at the thief. Myrrh hopes it's just water in that cup.

She steps into the room. A man near her end of the table notices her and elbows the middle-aged woman beside him. Hair pinned up in an elaborate set of curls, the woman stops speaking and gives Myrrh a slow and judging once-over. Myrrh wonders, briefly, if the woman is responsible for the contents of her wardrobe. Glint did say her clothing was selected by one of his associates.

Silence descends on the table.

"Ah, our newest recruit. Everyone, meet Myrrh. Hawk's protégé."

Glint's stare commands her forward. Myrrh doesn't feel like a protégé, and certainly not like someone meant to lead these people, but she steps to the table and lays her hand on the back of an unoccupied chair. Glint shakes his head, an almost imperceptible motion. His eyes flick to the empty spot on his right.

Running her finger along the chair back as if she were simply inspecting its quality, Myrrh inclines her head toward the group and glides forward. Heads turn to follow her progress. Eyes seem to pierce the velvet gown, looking for the grubber thief hidden beneath.

Myrrh raises her chin. Showing insecurity in front of a room of career criminals is a sure way to end up knifed in the back. They need to respect her, or better yet, fear her. She turns narrowed eyes on them, imagining herself not in a rustling bushel of fabric, but in the ratty woolen thief's garb she's worn every night as she's worked her way from middling pickpocket to one of the most successful freelancers south of Third Bridge. While these people were taking orders, she was cutting her own path. She is twice the rogue they are.

It seems to work. Conversation resumes, the woman with the elaborate hair deliberately turning away and mentioning something to her neighbor about the price of teakwood carvings from the Sovild witches.

She hears the soft rush of air as Glint exhales. He turns back to Nab. "If you wouldn't mind, tell Tep we're ready for more wine and the first course."

Nab jumps up, not at all bothered by being named errand boy for the party. If anything, he looks honored to be chosen. Myrrh sighs. Why doesn't the little flea give *her* that kind of respect? She's been putting food in that skinny belly for the better part of three years. Maybe she ought to stop, let him scratch out his own meals for a change.

Except she'd break down at the first glimpse of the dull-eyed hunger he wore when she and Hawk found him begging. All knobby knees and too-large eyes, he looked just a day or two short of starvation. He still hasn't outgrown those hungry years. Not yet.

The boy returns followed by Tep, who makes a round of the table, refilling goblets. Including Nab's. Oh well. As he's said many times, she's not his mother.

"So," Glint says in a conversational tone.

The room instantly stills. All eyes turn to him.

He raises his glass. "To Hawk."

"Hawk," everyone choruses.

Dizziness strikes her. Myrrh manages to tip a sip of wine down her throat before setting her goblet down with a clack. Glint could have told her this was a wake as much as a dinner.

Then again, if he'd warned her, could she have walked in here with the same confidence?

Around the table, thieves start telling stories of scores and heists that Hawk set up. There are tales of drunken celebrations too, and none of them sound like the serious man who pushed her so hard to learn the craft. Myrrh holds her own stories inside. These people don't need to hear how Hawk went hungry one week so she could eat when pickings were thin. Or how he handed over his dagger and told her to never, ever let the edge get dull. None of them knew the man like she did. Not even Glint. And they don't deserve to meet him now.

She stiffens when Glint touches her hand. The man leans close to her ear. "Eat," he whispers. "Hawk taught you to hide emotions, right? Food is an excellent distraction."

A small roast bird sits on a little plate in front of her. When did it appear? While she was staring into space, fighting tears over Hawk's loss? Glint is right. She's dangerously close to showing what she really feels.

The smell of herbs and butter and meat finally registers. Myrrh's mouth starts to water. She picks up a fork and knife and examines the bird. A quail? Where to start? She punctures the golden skin over the breast, feels it crinkle around her fork. The bird is so small, it's hard to work the knife in.

Glint nudges her under the table with his foot. Rather deliberately, he picks up the quail in both hands and tears off a bite with his teeth. He winks as he chews, and Myrrh glances down the table. At least half the guests have likewise abandoned their manners. One, a balding man with knuckles the size of walnuts, pulls a wing off his bird and actually slings it across the table at a woman with a gem-studded eye patch.

The woman laughs and shrugs. "More for me." She picks up the wing and sucks meat from the bone.

When she looks back at Glint, he raises an eyebrow, eyes twinkling as if to say, "I told you so."

Nab falls into the conversation much more easily than Myrrh does. Maybe she's still off-balanced by the reminder of Hawk's loss. Glint leans forward and points the tip of his knife at each of the thieves, introducing them to her. Mink, Resh, Lavi—she's the one with the eye patch—Scowl, obvious because of his expression, Nyx, Shiny, and Gray. Myrrh nods, matching names to faces in her memory.

She's glad for the distracting parade of courses that lands in front of her. More meat. Cheeses. A fruit divided into sections that Glint calls an *orange.* She's not sure if he's teasing her. It seems as ludicrous as calling apples *reds* and *greens.* But the taste is divine. A hundred little pouches of juice release their nectar over her tongue when she bites down. If her life from here on out is filled with stupidly named fruit and a table full of swindlers who don't care how much food they spill on their fancy clothing, she thinks she can be happy.

Dessert arrives. Nab groans in pleasure to see the little plate with another chocolate tart like he sampled a few nights ago.

Partway through the course, Glint takes a deep breath, gathering attention without needing to speak.

Myrrh's heart hammers in her chest. Is he going to bring up his plans for her? She hasn't really had the chance to make an impression one way or the other.

"There's one more thing," he says.

Myrrh lays down her fork.

"We've been growing in strength for months. Preparing our moves. One of our founders is dead. He can't be replaced."

Glint's gaze passes over her as he makes eye contact with the rest of his leadership. Her neck tenses as she forces her eyes off her plate.

"But we can honor him. We can make this organization everything Hawk wanted it to be. Starting tonight."

Her brow knits. That doesn't sound like a preamble for explaining her promotion.

"Originally, I expected to wait to make this move, but certain...actions"—he flicks his gaze to her—"have changed some priorities."

Actions? Myrrh cocks her head.

"For reasons I won't go into, Porcelain Hand has denied us access in and out of Maire's Quarter. Obviously, if we want to keep making the kinds of scores that fund this sort of debauchery"—he gestures to the table and the remains of the feast—"we need to secure that tunnel."

"Are you talking about claiming territory?" asks Resh, the bald man who threw some of his dinner at Lavi. "Thought that wasn't the sort of thing we bother with."

Glint stands, presses the point of his steak knife into the table, lightly supporting it with his index finger and thumb. "I'm not talking about scratching out turf. I'm talking about a quick, decisive strike. We're going to gut the syndicate, tear out its heart, and put our own regime in place. A coup. Before the sun rises, we'll be kings and queens of Lower Fringe. And if we do it right, we'll be unassailable."

Murmurs rise from the guests. Though Glint shows no doubt outwardly, Myrrh can feel it coming off of him. Regardless of what he claims, this *is* a strike intended to claim turf. A change in the strategy that lured these people to the organization in the first place. He's probably debating whether the change needs more justification, weighing that against the weakness that explaining himself could indicate.

"Everyone able to get their men and women into place for a strike?"

He looks around the table as if daring someone to refuse.

Finally, a grin splits Lavi's face. "Nines in the hand. This sounds like the most fun we've had since you pinched that sixing signet ring."

Chapter Nineteen

Why didn't Glint mention the problems with the thieves' path earlier? If he wants her to make a good impression, why put her off-balance with surprises? And furthermore, if he didn't want her to cause trouble with Porcelain Hand during her "audition," he ought to have warned her.

Anyway, she can't help her singing nerves as she heads up the stairs to prepare for the operation. She's been paired with Mink, the middle-aged woman with the curled hair and superior attitude. The choice almost makes Myrrh think that Glint is setting her up to fail. But that can't be the case, can it?

When she hears his footsteps following her up the stairs, she turns.

"Is the access tunnel the only reason you decided to go after Porcelain Hand?"

He stops one stair below her, his eyes even with hers. Shadows sketch the strong lines of his features. "Are you questioning the decision?"

"Only the motive."

"It wasn't going well."

"What wasn't?"

"Your introduction. Half of them had dismissed you as unimportant."

Myrrh is glad for the lack of candlelight in this part of the stairwell. Shame fills her cheeks.

"How did you know that?"

"I know my people." He cups her elbow, urging her to continue up the stairs. "But it wasn't your fault. Let's talk elsewhere."

She expects another conversation in the sitting room but then remembers that Glint sent Nab and Tep up there with a decanter of heavily watered wine and a set of dice. Instead, he guides her to his room. Inside, he offers her the lone chair at the table. After pacing for a moment, he drags over the chair from the writing desk and sets it opposite her.

He faces her over the low candle burning between them. "In truth, the problem is with my leaders, not you. That's part of why I brought up Hawk. To watch their reactions. They aren't ready to consider anyone else as my second-in-command, as it were. Mink—"

"No need to rub it in. It was pretty clear what she thinks of me."

"And does she have any reason for that opinion?"

"No," she says, rolling her eyes. "That's the problem. She thinks I'm a no-good grubber from the Spills. Looked at me like this was my first sixing time out of Rat Town."

He stares at her, gaze penetrating. "Some of that's true, isn't it?"

Abruptly, she's so angry she could spit. "I *chose* the freelance life. And I worked my way up without the help of a syndicate. I'm a sixing good thief, Glint."

He sighs and leans back. "I know."

"Then why are you defending her?"

"I'm guessing after what happened during the spice theft that you've never killed someone before. I don't mean to bring up a sore subject, but we need to get that out in the open."

That shuts her up for a minute. "I'm a thief, not an assassin."

"Doesn't matter. Whether you're a smuggler or a privateer or an informant for the wrong people, eventually it will happen. Like back in that sewage tunnel on your first job with me. You came out alive. But so did the men chasing you."

"I wasn't trying to kill them. Just slow them down so I could hop the barge."

"Would you have been safer if you'd left two bodies behind? They could have caught you halfway across the river."

She shrugs. "Maybe."

"Point is—"

"Point is, you seem bound and determined to put me down here. Not a full day after you said you wanted me to take over your organization."

He pulls the glass stopper from his decanter of whiskey and pours a splash into the tumbler. Myrrh shakes her head when he offers it, though the sharp fumes smell pretty good right now.

"If you'll let me finish...the point is, Mink cut her way into Haven's inner circle by being one of the best assassins ever to work in Ostgard. She might have killed her way straight to the kingpin position if I hadn't enticed her away. Not only that, she's a passable thief besides. So she has every right to be arrogant, and I don't blame her for looking at you and seeing a wide-eyed girl on a sightseeing trip."

Myrrh's toes crack as she curls them inside her lace-up boots. She clamps her teeth over her words and settles for hitting him with her hardest glare.

"You can be mad all you like. I'm just telling you the truth. Lately, you've proved everything Hawk said about you. Including the part about how you could use a little humility. A little *less* confidence in some situations."

She plants her palms on the table, preparing to stand and leave. Glint calmly leans forward and grabs her wrist, holding her in place. "I paired you with Mink because it's the only way she'll accept you. She has to see you in action."

"Another test."

"Do you want the job or not?"

And abruptly, she realizes she wants it more than anything. She nods.

"For the record, I haven't killed anyone either. Not on purpose anyway."

"What? You?"

"Which is precisely why I need people like Mink. Back on the stairs, you asked about my motive. Our access to Maire's Quarter is important, but alone, that's not a reason to depose a whole syndicate. Porcelain Hand will go down tonight because my organization needs to work an operation with you. They need you to be part of our biggest score yet."

"Taking down Porcelain Hand is a score?"

"More or less. Regardless of what I've claimed, there *are* benefits to owning criminal rights to a city district. It just wasn't part of the plan until tonight."

He's still got her wrist in an iron grip. When she glances down at it, he slowly releases her.

"So I tag along with Mink and hope to impress her?"

"Is that the kind of person you are? Someone who tags along and hopes to impress."

"No."

"Then that was a rhetorical question. Take charge where you can, but please don't forget what got the woman this far. There's a chance you might learn something."

She stands and pushes her chair into the table. "I better go get ready."

He nods, sipping his whiskey. When she's nearly at the door, he speaks.

"Planning to cut that dress off?"

Myrrh lays a hand on the door latch but doesn't open it. "Would you kindly unbutton me?"

Glint chuckles as he crosses the room. Quick fingers work down the row of little buttons. As soon as he's finished, Myrrh yanks the door open and stalks out without looking back.

***

"Wait," Myrrh whispers, laying a hand on Mink's arm. Mink halts, crouching near the edge of the rooftop and peering down at the fog-cloaked street far below.

The older woman is a different person than the would-be high-society matron that sat at Glint's dinner table. She's clad in tight-fitting clothing, not leather, but some sort of light weave that stretches and moves with her form. Her only armor is a hardened-leather bracer on her left arm. Her hair pulls severely away from her face, not a strand escaping the braid that runs down her back.

At least a dozen knives are strapped to her boots, thighs, and hips. Myrrh suspects there are many more hidden on her body.

"Yes?" Mink says. There's no annoyance in her tone. Tonight is all about business. And whether or not she respects Myrrh's skills, she's wise enough not to give emotion any space to work. Myrrh makes a mental note to remember that.

"We should use the glimmer."

"Premature," Mink says. "We have ten blocks before we need to drop down."

The woman starts to leave, utterly silent as she stalks along the rooftop's edge. Though Myrrh envies the woman her stealth, she's glad for the faintly creaking leather protecting her body. Glint's talk of assassins and killing has put her on edge. Most of Myrrh's gigs have been far different than this. Finding hidden access to dockside warehouses. Creeping onto barges when the guards are looking the other way. Making off with a cask of brandy here, a string of pearls there.

Tonight, they aren't after petty cash from a merchant's saddlebags. They're a shadow army ready to drop through roof hatches, rise from cellars, dive through windows at precisely the same time. Glint's order is to avoid violence wherever possible. But scuffles are inevitable. Their targets won't be hired guards lazily swiping at thieves making off with small prizes. They'll be hardened criminals fighting for their homes.

Myrrh shakes her head, jumps forward, and catches hold of Mink's wrist. This time, the woman's temper shows in the narrowing of her eyes and the way she jerks her arm away.

"It's a gut feeling," she says. "Cutpurse's intuition. There's trouble on the next roof."

Regardless of whether the woman will heed her warning, Myrrh isn't going to advance without the resin. Glint mentioned Mink's arrogance. That alone is reason for Myrrh to be cautious. She tucks a hand into her collarbone pocket and pulls out the packet of wax paper. As she slips the resin into her cheek, Mink stares as if shocked a mere girl would defy her advice. Lip curled, she turns to continue her advance.

A hiss slices the air just right of the women. Mink dives flat to the rooftop and kicks out Myrrh's knees. Myrrh hits. Hard.

"Sixes," Mink hisses. "Crossbow. Next roof."

A breath later, the woman has somehow rolled to her feet. She's a liquid shadow sliding over the rooftop. Like breeze-blown smoke, she approaches the gap between buildings. With a flick of her wrist, a knife flies across to the next rooftop, blade winking in the dull light of the cloud-hazed moon.

On the other roof, someone sucks in a rattling breath. Glimmer floods Myrrh's body in time for her to see a man where moments ago there was only a shadow hunkering in the shelter of a rooftop water tank. He clutches his neck, pulls out Mink's knife, releases a gush of blood.

A heartbeat later, he falls in a heap.

Myrrh blinks. Is he dead? Just like that? She waits for the sudden rush of guilt, but unlike with the young man on the barge, this kill was in self-defense. She feels only relief that Mink acted so quickly.

The woman motions her forward as she reaches into a pocket. The crinkle of paper tells Myrrh she's unwrapping her dose of resin.

"Good instincts," the older woman says. There's no apology in her voice, but no shame about being wrong either. Myrrh notices crow's feet in the corners of the woman's eyes. What is it like, coming into her middle years with a trail of bodies behind her? Does she plan to work as an assassin into old age? It's not something Myrrh has thought about, but seeing the woman work, she wonders whether Mink's life will be hers someday.

"Good throw," Myrrh responds. One at a time, they dart over the plank bridge that has been laid between the buildings.

Mink pauses briefly over the body. "I don't like that he shot at us. No reason for Porcelain Hand to know we're coming. No reason for him to mark us as enemies from that distance."

"You think they got news of our operation?"

"I don't know. We should be careful."

"Seems too late to call things off."

"Agreed." Mink peers over the rooftops, eyes searching for more threats. "Glint is pulling no punches tonight. The whole organization is in motion."

"Seems like an awfully big operation to put together in a matter of hours."

The older woman smirks. "That's one thing you'll learn about Glint. He might make quick decisions, but he's never as spontaneous as he seems. He may not have planned to take down Porcelain Hand before the altercation over the access to Maire's Quarter. But you can be certain he'd figured out *how* to do it just in case. Contingencies, you might say."

"But he didn't mention a contingency for turning back if the operation looks sketchy."

Mink shakes her head. "No half measures when Glint's calling the shots. It's something of a philosophy with him. Give someone the option of retreating and they sometimes lack the...urgency for success."

"So this guy..." Myrrh nudges the body with her toe. "Maybe he just had a twitchy trigger finger."

"Maybe so." The older woman sighs. "Stay sharp anyway."

Myrrh nods.

"And I meant what I said before. Good instincts. Even better that you listened to them."

After another few blocks, the thieves' path descends a fire escape to wind through a network of narrow alleys near the border between Lower Fringe and the Crafter's District. The smell of leather tanneries and cloth dyers infiltrates the streets, woven with the more distant stench of Smeltertown. Rats, absent in the more upscale region of Lower Fringe, scrabble over stone as they flee the women's advance.

Light leaks from the edges of shutters, but none reaches down to the streets. Still, with the glimmer, it's bright as day even in the trash-heaped corners of the alleys.

Myrrh knows they're close when Mink slows her pace. Glimmer-enhanced, the woman's motions are razor sharp. Deadly. When she creeps forward, it's almost unnatural looking.

"Here," Mink whispers, pointing to a shuttered window that looks no different than any of the past dozen they've walked beneath. That was another good reason for Glint to pair her with the older woman, Myrrh realizes. She's too new to the area to move about without some sort of map.

"Now we wait?"

The assassin nods.

Backs to the wall, they take positions on either side of the window. After a while, Mink rises up on tiptoes and slips a blade along the edge of the shutter. Making sure she can flip the latch open from the outside.

The night's chill begins to sink through Myrrh's clothing. She suppresses a shiver, thinking of Mink's thin garb and the woman's apparent indifference to the cold.

Both women stiffen when a clatter erupts from a heap of rubbish around fifty paces away. There's a squeak and a yelp, and then a stray dog trots by, casting them a disgusted glance as if it's their fault the hunter missed its prey.

Time crawls on, and Myrrh thinks of the rest of the organization. As best she understands, there are close to fifty talented thieves and killers poised outside gambling dens and Porcelain Hand safe houses across the district. All waiting for the signal.

Finally, it comes. A whistle from four or five blocks away. Mink makes a ring with the tips of her middle finger and thumb, presses them into her mouth, and blows hard, a piercing note that will carry the order to the next location. A heartbeat later, she stabs her blade through the crack at the edge of the shutter, throws open the latch, yanks open the shutter.

The glimmer makes Myrrh's movements perfect as she snatches the windowsill, pulls herself up in one smooth motion, and dives into the room. Mink follows, smooth as an eel.

It's a kitchen. Back of a tavern where Porcelain Hand runs the portion of their enterprise that extorts "protection" payments from nearby tradespeople.

The room is empty. Kitchen's closed for the night because everyone's eaten by this hour, and all they really care about now is getting drunk. As Myrrh and Mink agreed earlier, they split up and approach the door to the barroom along opposite walls.

Myrrh stiffens when a barmaid backs through the door, a tray of dirty tankards in her hands. The girl laughs, the giggle obviously fake and intended to avoid angering the drunk who just catcalled her.

Mink draws herself upright when the door swings shut. She slips a small blade from a sheath on her thigh. Myrrh closes her eyes.

Fortunately, the girl doesn't notice either of them. With an exhausted sigh, she slings the tray onto the kitchen counter, tankards clinking.

There's a washtub full of dirty water against the back wall. The girl gives it a disgusted glance. Curls her lip. Reluctantly, she picks up the first tankard and shuffles forward to start washing it.

Myrrh nods at the door to the barroom and starts creeping forward. With a considering glance at the distracted barmaid, Mink shrugs, then nods. They approach the door together. The assassin switches blades, opting for something with more exposed steel, then counts to three on her fingers.

The women burst into the room, the sudden noise of drunken patrons causing the girl to yelp. Water splashes, no doubt the sound of the tankard taking a swim in the washtub. Myrrh shuts out her awareness of the barmaid. The threats are in the front room.

Just two people react with anything but bleary stares. A man with a livid scar on his neck jumps up, grabbing for a knife at his hip while the bartender, a strong woman with keen eyes, reaches beneath the bar. For a crossbow, Myrrh assumes.

Everyone else tries to hide behind their drinks. A few raise hands in surrender. Whatever's going on here, they just want to finish their beers and go home.

Myrrh springs for the scarred man, the glimmer cold in her veins. She lands a precise kick to his elbow before he gets a grip on his knife. At the same time, a throwing knife somehow appears in Mink's hand. A heartbeat later, it's embedded an inch deep in the wood beam just above the bartender's head.

"I don't think I need to tell you that I missed on purpose," Mink says.

The woman's hands emerge from beneath the bar. Empty. Fingers splayed.

"How about you?" Myrrh asks, laying her dagger against the man's throat.

"I got no quarrel," he says, raising his hands.

She pulls the knife from his belt and tosses it under another table.

"Name?" she asks.

"Tom. Look, I'm just here for a drink. Got startled is all."

Myrrh looks at Mink, shakes her head.

"Sit," she says to the man. "You can leave once our business here is concluded."

"How about you?" Mink asks the bartender. "What's your name?"

"Depends on who you ask," the bartender says, eyes spitting with anger.

Everyone on the operation has memorized a list of names: the roster of Porcelain Hand members worth recruiting. The others, the deadweight that has hobbled the syndicate for years, will be allowed to surrender their weapons and walk out of the district. Even if they were to organize—which Glint is sure they lack the initiative to do—they represent no threat.

Many of the worthy recruits will accept the generous signing bonus Glint has tucked away. Those who refuse won't see the sunrise. Myrrh has a sinking feeling the bartender may be one of those.

"I go by V to most. Tuck to my friends."

Myrrh remembers the name, clear as if she'd just read the list. Glint's notes list V as something of a mastermind in the protection scheme.

"Do you know why we're here, Tuck?" she asks.

"You ain't my friend," the woman says.

"Perhaps we can change that." Myrrh stalks toward the big woman. A glance at Mink tells her the assassin has an eye on Tom as well. "I get the feeling you recognize the value of talented—and wealthy—allies."

The bartender shows her palms, then sets her hands flat on the bar. "I'm listening."

Chapter Twenty

Myrrh can't shake the feeling that something's wrong. She and Mink escort their captive back, sticking to alleys for discretion but avoiding the thieves' paths that wind over rooftops and up and down ladders. The bartender, V, agreed to be blindfolded. Not that she had much choice. Myrrh keeps a hand on the woman's sturdy arm, careful not to jerk too hard on her bound wrists.

Fog pools in the alleyways and muffles the low din of the city. As they turn another corner, feet scuffing on rain-slick cobblestones, Mink steps closer.

"It was too easy," the assassin says.

Myrrh was thinking the same. The tavern was supposed to be headquarters for a major arm of Porcelain Hand's operations. They scarcely met resistance. She nods, eyes alert. Where lamplight gleams off wet stone, the glimmer-sight makes the street appear to smolder.

"Any comment?" Mink asks, prodding their captive's shoulder with the butt of one of her knives. "Is it usual that you were the only competent person working the tavern?"

The bartender shrugs. "I have many things to say. But not until I hear your offer."

Mink turns her knife, presses the blade against the woman's neck. "You might not live that long."

The bartender laughs. “I said I’d make it worth your while to bring me on. Killing me now would squander a resource. And you still wouldn’t get answers.”

Mink pulls the blade away. “I hope for your sake that you’re right about your value. Our invitation can always be rescinded.”

As they near the river, the fog thickens. Streetlamps struggle to penetrate the haze, turning the world into shadows that would be impenetrable without the glimmer. As they wind through alleys, Myrrh glimpses figures paralleling their course. More of Glint’s associates, returning from their designated raids. They’re converging with the captives, but not to Glint’s new residence. There’s another safe house, less conspicuous than the building he’s setting up for his front as a merchant. Myrrh’s last task tonight is to fetch Glint once the operation is complete.

Sounds from the river drift through the night, the shouts of bargemen and the occasional clang of a bell. Myrrh can smell the Ost now. They’re close.

“You know the way to the rendezvous?” Mink asks.

“I’ll be with Glint.”

Mink’s lips thin. “Always best to have a contingency. The location is three blocks upriver from where we met tonight. Look for an alley with a lantern hanging from the wall halfway down.”

Myrrh nods. They’ve reached the street corner where she needs to split off. The assassin takes hold of the captive’s arm, her grip not as gentle as Myrrh’s was. Mink jerks the bartender away, and Myrrh sets off for Glint’s residence at a trot.

When she turns a corner onto the street that fronts the building, she freezes in her tracks. The front door hangs ajar. The windows are dark, not a hint of light leaking through the curtains. Myrrh forces herself to keep walking, passing by the door without staring. No sound comes from inside.

Sixes.

She turns the next corner, following the outer wall of the building where Glint's high window has a vantage on a slice of the waterfront. That, too, is dark.

A narrow alley cuts across the back of the building. Myrrh slips down it. Around twenty paces from the street, a ground floor window is cracked. On tiptoes, she peeks in.

A single lantern burns in the kitchen, adding to the smoldering glow from the oven.

The chef lies on the floor, legs splayed and arms outflung. He isn't moving. His cleaver rests a few inches from his fingertips, glinting in the red glow from the oven. She doesn't see blood but can't tell if he's breathing.

She waits for ten long breaths, listening. The only sounds are the low crackle of flames in the oven and the cooing of pigeons in the building's eaves. She pulls her dagger, nudges the window open. Lays hands on the windowsill and vaults up and through. An echo of her entrance into Porcelain Hand's tavern.

She runs in a crouch for the chef. Lays fingers on his neck. There's a steady but weak pulse. His eyelids flutter at her touch, but he doesn't wake. There's no sign of Tep.

Or Nab. It hits her all at once. Nab was here, safely tucked away in the sitting room to play dice with his new friend.

Myrrh's heart thuds as bile rises. She can't lose him, not so soon after Hawk.

It takes everything she has to force away rising panic. With a deep breath, she slips to the door leading to the dining room, cracks it, peers out.

Darkness fills the room. The dim light that falls through the front door is reflected faintly in the shards of glass that litter the floor. The table's been overturned, candles and pitchers and cutlery strewn.

It's quiet as a tomb. Myrrh slips forward, setting feet between crunching fragments of glass. Still no sounds from inside the building. Whatever happened here, it's over.

She should hurry to the rendezvous, get help. But she needs to know. What happened to Nab?

She takes the steps three at a time, dashing up to the fourth floor and the sitting room where she last saw the boy.

She stops in the doorway. The carafe lies on its side, watered wine spilled across the table. The dice are scattered, two on the floor, the rest on the table. The fire still crackles.

No bodies. At least she can hold on to hope that Nab is alive. But he's gone. Vanished.

Back against the wall, she slides down and covers her face with her hands.

***

The safe house is a tenement building designed to house servants for the merchants and traders and shipping magnates who call Lower Fringe home. The captives—around fifteen members of Porcelain Hand—have been locked into individual apartments, windowless rooms that are barred from the outside. Lower-level members of the organization stand guard over each makeshift prison cell while Glint's leadership crowds into a ground-floor room.

Nyx, a slight man with shifty eyes and hair cut close to his scalp, paces.

His glance lands on Myrrh. "Thank you for the report. You can go."

Myrrh steps farther into the room. "I'm staying."

"Inner circle only."

"Nyx," Mink says. "It's okay."

The small thief glares at Myrrh, then shrugs and resumes his pacing. Silence gathers in the room while the thieves consider what Myrrh has told them.

After a moment, Mink pushes off the wall. "There's a body on a rooftop. A crossbowman ambushed us en route from Glint's to the tavern near the Crafter's District. Probably worth searching."

"Send someone," the big, bald thief, Resh, says.

The other thieves nod, and Mink steps into the hallway. She speaks in a low voice to someone, then returns and shuts the door behind her.

Resh clears his throat. "We'll want to search the residence."

"Better to do it in daylight." This from Lavi, the woman with the gem-studded eye patch. Except now, she's not wearing it, and Myrrh can't help but notice that neither of her eyes is damaged.

Myrrh meets Nyx's gaze, daring him to challenge her when she speaks. "Our captive, V. She knows something."

A rumble rises from Resh's throat. "Let's bring her down."

Mink leaves again, slipping out the door. While they wait, Myrrh crosses the room, edging around the table where no one sits, and takes up a spot with her back to the wall. She feels eyes on her, meets their stares, and confronts expressions in a range from calculating to dismissive.

The bartender enters the room with a glower on her face.

"Sit," Nyx says with a sneer. The orientation of the table means the woman will have her back to trained killers. Myrrh sees the hesitation on V's face, but the woman swallows her nerves and stalks to the table. She flops into a chair, props a heel on another seat, and turns a surly glare to the room. "I'm waiting for my offer."

"There's been a delay," Mink says.

"Then why are we talking?"

Nyx steps forward, pulls a knife, and smacks it onto the table. He stares at the woman. "We took down your syndicate in one strike. Nabbed everyone who matters and sent the rest packing."

"Everyone?" V asks, a smirk touching her face.

"So you're aware that five of your inner circle were missing tonight." Mink spins a blade over her fingers as she speaks.

"I might be aware of that."

"You couldn't have known we were coming," Nyx says. "Which means your men didn't flee."

"That's quite an assumption. Perhaps we knew your plans. Expected a strike and sent five of our best away to rally the retaliation. The counterattack could be moving in on this building as we speak."

Mink snorts. "You're a decent liar, but we've got you on this one. *We* didn't even know we planned to take you down tonight. Not until just before the operation."

V laughs. "All right. Got me there. So, want to tell me why my offer's delayed? I expected to meet your leader. Unless..." She pointedly looks around the room, seeming to evaluate and reject each thief as capable of leading an organization.

No one answers her query. One by one, Glint's associates cross their arms over their chests.

"Look," V says finally. "I get it. Porcelain Hand is gutted. Done. Dead and buried. Even if those few who escaped your net come back, they won't be able to reconstitute our organization. I need somewhere to go, but I've got my pride, you know. I ain't signing on without some tempting promises."

Myrrh glances around the room. This stonewalling isn't getting them anywhere. She steps forward. "You'll have a position of leadership. Equal in rank to everyone here. Freedom to organize operations in the Crafter's District. You can take twenty percent directly out of the proceeds from your work, plus the usual stipend."

The rest of Glint's leadership stares. She can hear their unspoken questions. Where in the sixing world did she get the authority to offer that?

Nyx opens his mouth to protest, but Lavi elbows him in the ribs.

"Now that's better. Wasn't so hard, was it?" V takes her heel off the chair, sits forward, and meets Myrrh's eyes. "You're right that we didn't expect you. Was just bad luck. We got word that Slivers was making an offensive in our territory. Didn't know their plans, whether it was a heist or a grab for turf or what. Just knew they were moving in with heavy hitters and not a single attempt to negotiate an operation in our area. You missed capturing our best people because we sent them to lead a counteroffensive."

"When?" Resh asks.

"Early evening. We expected results by now."

"So you have nothing to do with the attack on one of our safe houses?" Myrrh says.

V raises an eyebrow. "No disrespect, but I've got no sixing idea who you people are. Much less where you have safe houses."

Myrrh swallows the rush of cold rising from her gut. Slivers? What are they doing so far from Rat Town?

She can't help the thoughts that crowd in. Hawk was betrayed in Rat Town. For that matter, so was she. And if Glint hadn't stepped in, she'd probably be just as dead as Hawk. And now the same people who did him in may have Glint and Nab.

A knock comes at the door. Mink yanks it open, admitting a thief who pants from exertion. "The rooftop. Wasn't Porcelain Hand."

"Slivers?" Resh asks.

The thief nods.

"You sure?"

Myrrh's heart sinks as the thief holds up a steel rod of the sort Slivers uses to pierce the cartilage in their members' upper ears. It's their syndicate's mark. No doubt about it.

Chapter Twenty-One

With the door firmly shut and barred, Myrrh and Lavi pick through the ruins of Glint's dining room. The heavy drapes are drawn over the windows, shutting out the morning sun. Myrrh is glad for the dimness. She hasn't slept, and her eyes are full of sand. She peers around the back side of the table, looking for clues about what happened. As far as she can tell, tipping the table was a show of violence for the sake of it.

Nyx emerges from the kitchen, shaking his head and tearing—disrespectfully, in Myrrh's opinion—at a hunk of bread with his teeth.

Lavi lays a hand on the edge of the sharply slanted tabletop. "So let me review. Porcelain Hand gets word of the Slivers incursion. They respond, results still unknown—"

"Well, we do know that the interception wasn't completely successful," Nyx interrupts. "Because Slivers came here."

"You sure it was Slivers that did this?" Lavi asks.

"A strange coincidence otherwise," Myrrh interjects.

Lavi scoots broken glass and the stump of a candle into a pile with her foot. "The Queen of Nines plays many strange games with chance. I don't want to believe anything without proof."

"In any case," Nyx says around a bite of food, "Glint was expecting Myrrh to report in on the operation, so he was probably careless when they—Slivers or some unknown party—came knocking at the front door. Does that sound about right?"

"Seems right to me," Lavi says. She picks up a fork. "This is nice silver. Who pinched it for him anyway?"

Myrrh takes a deep breath, feels her nostrils flare. For these people, this is just work. Glint is their leader, but they aren't family. Not like her and Nab.

"We get anything from the chef?" Lavi asks. Shortly after Myrrh reported the break-in, a trio of thieves was sent to either get the chef to safety or to see to the disposal of his body. Apparently, he'd survived.

"He claims he heard a noise from the dining room and started for the door. Remembers nothing after though. He took a major blow to the back of his head."

Myrrh sighs. Likely, someone came in the same window she did. It was too easy, just like their takedown of Porcelain Hand. Of all people, she would've expected Glint to be more cautious. Especially after Hawk. And what are the chances of Slivers choosing to strike tonight, both weakening Porcelain Hand and catching Glint during a rare moment of distraction? Is she missing something?

"Let's go up," Lavi says.

They take the staircase together. Myrrh stops at the second-floor landing, staring in shock at the ruins of the door that has been locked since she arrived. The jamb is splintered, and nothing but scraps of wood hang from the door hinges.

Inside the room, light falls through gauzy curtains, showing overturned crates and looted barrels. Bolts of cloth have been dragged across the floor, and the air smells chokingly of heavy perfume. She spots the shattered flask of scented oil after a moment's searching.

Nyx snorts. "So much for our stash. Well, the biggest one. The proceeds from all our hard work. I suppose we can be glad they couldn't carry everything..."

Lavi just shakes her head and continues up the stairs. When they reach the third floor, Myrrh steps into the corridor. "I'll start here; will you take the fourth?"

Nyx shrugs. "Don't suppose it matters. Sure."

Myrrh's boots whisper on the slates as she hurries down the hall. She starts at the end, hesitating for just a breath before slipping through the double doors into Glint's room. The covers have been pulled off the bed and now lie in a heap beside it. Wardrobe doors and dresser drawers hang open. Papers litter the floor around the writing desk.

Interestingly, though, the locked drawer on the desk remains closed. Myrrh crosses the room and runs a finger over the wood surrounding the little drawer. Gouges mar the wood where the abductors tried to force the lock, but they seem to have given up. Why? Did they run out of time? Decide they had enough loot for one night?

One of the many pockets sewn into her leathers holds her lockpicks. Myrrh's neither the best nor the worst at opening locks, but she shoves a pair of pins into the keyhole and hopes. With a deep breath, she starts fishing for the tumblers.

It's not a complicated lock. Within a minute or two, she feels a click as it disengages.

She slides the drawer open, not sure what she intends to find. A clue about why the Slivers struck? A notion of the connection between the raid on Glint's residence and Hawk's death? Something else in his correspondence that could point her to Nab's location?

Her hand falls on an oval of smooth metal. She pulls it out. A locket.

Unable to help herself, she thumbs the catch. The pendant flips open, showing a picture of an attractive woman dressed in finery that looks almost old-fashioned. She looks sad.

Myrrh swallows the strange emotion prompted by the glimpse into his personal life. She had no reason to believe he was unattached. It's just...surprising.

She sets the locket aside and pulls out a sheaf of papers.

The first few are a series of unsigned letters, observations on flow of trade along the River Ost. Records of which merchants and cartels have control over which types of goods. Though she doesn't recognize the handwriting, the choice of words reminds her of Hawk. Maybe some of these letters led them to the discovery of a faction moving against the Maire.

Other sheets detail locations—taverns, inns, gambling dens, and so forth—by street name or proximity to well-known buildings and intersections. Beside each, Glint has written down names of syndicates that control the locations and, or so it seems, the key players working there. Other notes record defenses and the number of syndicate members typically staffing each location.

It's a glimpse into Glint's so-called contingencies. Their organization was able to move on Porcelain Hand with no knowledge because of records like this. He's spent months amassing detailed knowledge of his enemies, even if he never planned to use much of it.

The next paper catches her eyes because it's been crumpled and flattened.

The handwriting is different than either the script she's decided must be Hawk's or that which she thinks is Glint's. It reads:

Your demands are not acceptable. We had a deal. Quell this threat to my authority, and I'll keep the rest of my bargain. Regardless of the ill will that taints our relationship, you can trust me in that.

Yours,

No name is signed. None is necessary. The Maire's seal is stamped at the bottom of the paper.

Myrrh feels as if she's standing on shifting sand. Glint has a *deal* with the Maire? He knows the man personally?

She blinks as she reads the note again. Is there something she's not understanding here?

The fact that the paper has been crumpled suggests anger. Maybe Glint contacted the Maire, thinking he could warn the man about the plot. Maybe he then tried to pressure the man for concessions once he proved that he could help the Maire keep his title. But that still doesn't explain the comment about their relationship.

She runs a hand through her hair. It's not like she hasn't been lied to before. Betrayed by people she thought she could trust. But not like this. Not when the life of an innocent boy is at risk.

Myrrh folds the note and tucks it into a pocket. She goes back to the rest of the papers, searching for a contingency for information on Slivers safe houses. Regardless of what Glint has been up to, it still seems almost certain the Rat Town syndicate took him and the boys. Finally, after rifling through another dozen sheets, she finds it. A list of Rat Town locations. The notes include names familiar to her from her time working as a grubber in Slivers territory.

"Anything?" Lavi asks from the door.

Myrrh jumps and turns to face the woman. Words form in her throat, but all of a sudden, she isn't sure whether she should tell these people anything. She isn't sure she *wants* them to go into Rat Town in force, not when she knows so little about what Glint was really up to. Not when Nab and Tep are hostages. She doubts Slivers would hesitate to kill the boys if they thought it would make Glint's people back off.

She needs to know more. Figure out where the captives are being held. Figure out *why* Slivers came for Glint. And she needs to do it without forcing the Rat Town syndicate to do anything rash. Quiet work. From the shadows. Tonight.

Myrrh shakes her head. "Nothing."

Lavi sighs. "Same. Just a bunch of ransacked rooms. But I don't think they were looking for anything in particular. Just opportunistic looting. The real prize was Glint."

"And Nab," Myrrh says. "They took two boys too."

She doesn't miss Nyx's eye roll. Lavi, at least, softens her expression.

"And Nab," the woman says. "Shall we go meet with the others? They should be done speaking with the prisoners and searching for a trail out of the district."

On the way out of the room, Myrrh folds the list of Slivers dens and stuffs it up her sleeve. She's been freelance for as long as she's been a thief.

Tonight, she'll work alone.

Chapter Twenty-Two

Myrrh is sitting at the now-righted table in Glint's dining room when a quiet knock comes at the door. Myrrh doesn't open it. Instead, she slides aside a small panel, opening a barred window.

An urchin with a grubby face stands outside. For a moment, hope tightens Myrrh's chest. An emissary from Slivers? Have they decided on a ransom? She's not sure she'd be eager to pay one for Glint, but no price would be too high for Nab's safe return.

"Tell your people Goosefoot wants to meet. Winks Tavern on the waterfront."

"Wait, who's Goosefoot?"

The child rolls his eyes. "Ask V if you can't figure it out." He runs off.

Porcelain Hand then. It's probably the missing members of the inner circle reaching out. She doesn't recognize the name from Glint's list of thieves to recruit though. Goosefoot is deadweight. Either way, she'll have to let the others know. It will be nice to do *something* better than dozing in the dining room of an empty mansion, waiting for evening to darken the streets.

Myrrh closes the panel, then makes a patrol of the ground floor to make sure all the windows are latched. The Slivers syndicate already has what it came for, but if any nearby grubbers have caught wind of last night's upheaval, they'll be eager for easy pickings.

Glint kept a key to the front door hanging from a post in the kitchen. She uses it to secure the bolt before pulling her cloak over her hair and trudging toward the other safe house.

Most of the leaders are sleeping in rooms upstairs, resting up in preparation for whatever they've planned for tonight. She rouses Mink and lets the older woman rouse the others. A few minutes later, they're gathered around the circular table in the downstairs room. Including, Myrrh is surprised to see, V.

The bartender nods when Myrrh repeats the message.

"One of ours."

"His position in your organization?" Resh asks.

"Shake's lackey. An incompetent thief, but good at following directions."

Myrrh watches the subtle shift of expressions on Glint's people. They'd reached the same conclusion she did about Goosefoot. Given their situation, no one wanted to waste time on demands from an underling. But Myrrh remembers seeing Shake on the list of worthy recruits. Near the top.

"I'll go to Winks," Mink says. "See what he has to say."

Resh nods. "I'll join you. We're in a difficult position. Need to consolidate here before we can hit Slivers, but since we don't know why they grabbed Glint, we don't know how urgent the situation is."

And Nab and Tep, Myrrh thinks. She says nothing.

"What else?" Nyx asks. "As long as we're awake"—he snarls at Myrrh—"might as well set a strategy for tonight."

"Would you rather she'd kept the message to herself?" Mink asks.

"I'd rather Glint hadn't brought on an amateur grubber just because he felt guilty for getting her daddy thief whacked."

Myrrh flares her nostrils but otherwise doesn't react. It doesn't matter what Nyx thinks. As far as she can tell, he's cruel for the sake of it.

Resh's face is stony as he turns to the smaller man. He slowly scoots back his chair, stands, leans forward, and *looms.* "I'm not Glint. Not calling the shots here. But I am certain he would evict you from this organization for those words." The bald man turns to Myrrh. "But our uncivilized friend does bring up a point. We assumed someone in Slivers was responsible for Hawk's unfortunate end. And now they've taken Glint."

"And Nab," she says softly.

Resh's face gentles. "And Nab. And the cook's lad. Forgive me. With your experience in Rat Town, can you think of a reason? Something that might help us retaliate and recover our allies?"

Myrrh isn't sure what to say. After seeing that note from the Maire, she isn't sure about anything. Except her need to find out what happened.

"Not yet. But that is one advantage of being an *amateur grubber.*" She glares briefly at Nyx. "You don't need my help consolidating in Lower Fringe. And with the big players moving, I doubt many people will pay attention to a small-time thief skulking through the Rat Town alleys. I'm leaving at dusk."

Resh nods. "A good plan."

"Before I go," she says, "I'd like to talk to the chef myself. See if he remembers anything strange from the last few days."

Lavi tips her chair back. "I'll say this for Glint—he inspires loyalty. Sixing cook has been working himself to death trying to get us to eat. Says keeping us fed and strong is the only thing he can do to help his young master." She gestures with her chin toward the back wall of the room. "He's in the kitchen down the hall."

"Thanks." Myrrh slides back her chair and slips through the door.

The chef stands over a pot of boiling water, cutting potatoes. Each chunk splashes as it tumbles into the water. He scarcely glances at her as she steps into the room. Exertion has reddened his face more than usual, and sweat dampens his hairline.

"After a blow to the head like that, don't you think you should be resting?" she asks.

"Can't. They have the young master."

"I never learned your name," Myrrh says as she steps up beside him. She pulls a potato from a basket, plunges it into a bucket of lukewarm water to scrub off the dirt.

"It's Bernard, miss."

"Myrrh."

"I know. You told me before. And the young master couldn't speak two sentences without mentioning you."

The words might have made her smile a day ago. Now she isn't sure what to think.

"You mentioned earlier that you've been with Glint for a long time."

"I shouldn't have, miss. It wasn't my story to tell." He accepts a freshly scrubbed potato from her and begins to slice it to pieces.

"Why not?" Steam from the pot flows out the cracked shutters on the window overhead. It makes her think of the window in Glint's kitchen and the damage this man took for his "young master." What did Glint do to inspire such loyalty? It doesn't quite fit with her new picture of a man who kept secrets, lied to her about a relationship with the leader of the city. The same city leader who ordered Hawk's capture—she assumes—and his execution. If being knifed in an alley, the Scythe's usual method, could even be named an execution.

"I'm sorry, miss. Myrrh. I'm not supposed to talk about it. Request of the young master himself."

She picks up another potato, brushes off dirt, and plucks out a sprouting eye before dunking it. Bernard grabs a dish from a shelf and pinches out a healthy measure of salt, sprinkling it into the pot. The water froths in response.

"The things you know might help us rescue him. Do you think Glint would allow an exception in this case?"

"I know nothing about this Slivers gang. My relationship with the young master is as a loyal chef."

"But you may know something about his relationship to the Maire."

Bernard's hesitation might have been easy to miss if she weren't looking for it. But she glimpses the paring knife held motionless against the rough skin of the potato, the flash of emotion across his face. He does know.

Bernard rises on tiptoe and nudges the shutter closed. Cut off from its exit, the trail of steam billows and begins to collect near the ceiling.

"I made the young master a promise," Bernard says with iron in his voice. "He wanted a new start."

"Did he work for the Maire? Or maybe his mother did. Is that why merchant henchmen murdered her?"

Bernard's hand trembles as he accepts the next scrubbed potato. Myrrh hates to put him through this, but she needs these answers.

"I can't say. He'd never forgive me."

She turns and leans the small of her back against the high counter. There has to be a way to get information from the man without making him feel as if he's betrayed Glint.

"Did *you* know the Maire before?" she asks. "Could Glint really object to you talking about your own history?"

Another chunk of potato splashes down, and droplets land on Bernard's forearm. He winces and pulls his hand back. A few deep breaths expand his chest while he thinks.

"Would knowing this *really* help recover the young master?" he asks. "On your honor, I need the truth."

Myrrh presses her lips together. "I can't say for certain. That's the truth. But we know so little right now. I really can't understand why Slivers would come after him. At this point, anything you can tell me has a chance of helping me find him and the boys."

Bernard sighs. "The Maire hired me as his personal chef when he was an upcoming merchant with a young wife..." He swallows, looking at his hands, the paring knife and half a potato cradled in his large palms. "And a little boy."

Myrrh doesn't remember hearing the Maire had a son...wait.

"Then Glint is his...?"

Bernard snaps his attention to the pot, begins slicing the potato like his very life depends on it. "I said nothing of the sort," he mutters.

***

Glint is the Maire's son. It knocks the breath from her every time she thinks the words. Myrrh paces back and forth across the second-floor storage room in Glint's home, shoving knives and piano wire and caltrops into the same canvas rucksack Glint used to carry weapons to their practice a few days ago. She wants to scream, wants to grab Glint by the shoulders and demand answers.

Why all the lies? What was his angle? Did Hawk die because of the man's fraud? She stops pacing and rests a hand against her forehead. Her shock at finding a picture of a woman in Glint's drawer seems so stupid now. A hidden girlfriend is the least of his deceptions.

The only thing that makes her think that maybe—*maybe*—there's a reasonable explanation for Glint's lies is Bernard's loyalty. The chef knows the truth of Glint's upbringing and follows him anyway. But it's not enough to convince her that he's anything short of a lowlife con artist.

Regardless of Glint's betrayals, she needs to find him so she can free Nab. And Tep. He's an obnoxious little flea, but as far as she knows, he's innocent. After that, Slivers can do what they want with Glint. She'll go back to the freedom of a grubber life. Never should have gotten tricked into believing she should be more anyway.

Are you thinking about this rationally? the traitorous voice in the back of her mind whispers. Doesn't he deserve a chance to explain? Maybe he had a good reason for hiding his past.

Or maybe he knew she'd slit his throat the moment she found out he was the son of the man who killed Hawk.

Myrrh grabs a throwing knife and hurls it at a wooden support post in the middle of the room. The blade clatters off the wood. She grits her teeth and clenches her fist.

Save it. Save the rage. That's what Hawk would say.

With a deep breath, Myrrh packs her anger down tight. It's a cold fire burning in her chest. She cinches the drawstring on the rucksack, drags it on, and drapes her cloak over it. Heads down the stairs and toward the door.

Evening light already paints the street red as she steps outside. The hour will soon arrive when the city's underworld will awake. And she will cut through it like a knife through the fog.

Chapter Twenty-Three

Rat Town closes around her like the embrace of a drunken friend who always seems a wrong word away from turning violent. Familiar in a way that makes her either want to cry in relief or empty her stomach. Streets of mud crisscross the district with no attempt at organization. Here and there, walkways of loose wood planks provide relief from the slimy muck. Hopelessly dilapidated, buildings lean against each other for support. Flames burn in dirty lanterns, the glass so begrimed that the light scarcely penetrates.

Home.

In all its filthy glory.

She slips down alleys and through dirt yards with her cloak's hood pulled forward to shadow her face. Her dagger's hilt presses hard against her palm. Slivers has so many dens in this warren of ramshackle shops and run-down inns that it's a roll of the dice to decide where to start. So she decides to go back to where this whole mess began. Rikson's Roost is the tavern where she secured the contract to rob the barge at First Docks, the operation where Warrell betrayed her. And it's the saloon where she heard the news of Hawk's capture just a few hours later. The establishment is more popular with freelancers than syndicate members. Better chance of picking up rumors and grabbing a drink without being noticed.

She hears the tavern from two blocks away. Voices shout over a piano that hasn't been tuned in years. Someone starts to sing, but it's cut short by the crash of breaking glass. Laughter follows.

As she approaches the door, she pulls her cloak tighter and ducks her head. The rucksack under her cloak will help disguise her slight stature, and as long as she keeps to herself, it's doubtful anyone will notice her. As she steps onto the long porch, a man sails out the open door, arms windmilling. He hits the street with a thump and slides through the muck. Moments later, he rolls to his feet and grins. Blood runs down his chin from the freshly knocked-out teeth.

"Sore loser." He cackles, then runs off, pockets clinking.

With a disgusted shake of his head, the bouncer dusts off his hands and heads back inside. Another figure steps into the doorway and makes a rude gesture into the night air. Myrrh assumes he's the gambler who just paid to have the other man thrown out.

When the man retreats, Myrrh steps into the doorway. She takes a deep breath, then regrets it as her nose fills with the smell of stale beer and body odor. Amazing how quickly she forgot that part.

She steps into the noise. At the far end of the bar, a couple of empty stools stand in relative darkness. She slips onto one, head down, hands loose on the bar top. A thousand scratches mar the wooden surface, memorializing years of knife fights and lonely patrons scratching out messages and doodles.

"What do you want?" The bartender stands sideways to her, eyes on the rest of the room.

"Ale, please."

He slaps his bar towel lightly on the counter by way of a response and stalks over to the tap. Shortly after, a foaming mug appears in front of her.

"Two coppers," the bartender says. He doesn't take his hand away until she planks the coins onto the bar.

Myrrh makes the mistake of looking up when she thinks he's moved off, and their eyes meet. She sees the flicker of surprise when he recognizes her.

With a subtle shake of her head, she pulls her dagger from its sheath and lays it on the bar top, fingers resting lightly on the hilt.

"I'm just here for information."

The man actually stammers, and before he manages to sort out his words, she feels a heavy hand on her shoulder.

Myrrh whirls, ducks away from the grip, and comes up with her blade at a muscular throat.

Growling, she raises her eyes to the face. And stiffens.

"Warrell."

The man's eyes plead while he raises his hands.

All the rage comes flooding back. The memories of his betrayal. The horror of hours spent as a helpless captive. "I'm surprised you have the guts to face me. Stupid, really." She presses the blade harder against his windpipe.

"W...wait. Myrrh." He takes a deep breath, flinches at the bite of her steel against his skin. "I need to...I'm...thank the Nines, you're here." His eyes flick to the bartender. "I'll have an ale as well. And another for Myrrh when she finishes the first."

Myrrh snarls. "There's no need. Warrell won't be drinking."

Warrell raises a hand toward her dagger, then seems to think better of it. Good. A few weeks ago, she might have hesitated to spill blood in the Roost. Not now.

"I know you think I betrayed you—"

"You sold me out for a lighter purse than I could make picking pockets in the night market."

"I can explain."

"Can you explain Hawk too? How much did you get for him?"

He shakes his head, and her dagger draws a bead of blood. "I did sell you out. But I had a good reason. You couldn't know, or the plan would have failed."

"I don't need to listen to this. Should I kill you here or outside?"

He blinks. "Glint had to trust you. It wouldn't have worked if you'd known. You wouldn't have been...convincing enough."

"What in the sixing pox are you talking about?" The veins in her temples are throbbing. Hadn't Glint said a similar thing? That Warrell had to believe that he'd thrown her to the hounds? Seems both these men were trying to use her to fool the other.

Another mug clacks against the bar top. Myrrh grits her teeth.

"Can we have that drink?" Warrell asks. "Once you hear what I have to say, I think you'll have a different opinion of me."

"Nothing you can say will convince me that it's okay that you abandoned me to a kingpin from Lower Fringe and betrayed Hawk to the Scythe."

He licks his lips. "There's someone else you should talk to then." He nods at the bartender who swallows and disappears into the back room.

Myrrh is caught between her desire for revenge and her curiosity. The little voice that pleaded for her to listen to Glint is now asking her to let this play out.

"Sit." She keeps her blade at his neck while Warrell slides onto a stool and wraps a large hand around his mug. Myrrh stays on her feet.

The moment drags on, her dagger against his throat, his eyes on the door where the bartender disappeared. If the other patrons are surprised to see her or concerned about her bared steel, none dare show it. Finally, another door opens, the exit into the set of rooms where Rikson's family lives.

"Myrrh!"

The sound of Nab's voice nearly makes her lose her grip on the dagger. She stares, mouth agape as he approaches. The boy's first steps are those of a child reunited with a beloved sibling. But the same transformation that began in Glint's home takes over, and he slows his walk to that of a surly teenager.

It's everything she can do not to laugh in relief at seeing him alive. She lowers her blade from Warrell's throat.

Nab steps close, eyes pleading. "They have Glint, Myrrh, and they're saying all these lies about him. You have to help!"

Myrrh swallows. She almost forgot how much Nab looked up to Glint and how much it will hurt him to learn the truth.

Warrell clears his throat. "So, are you ready to at least hear me out?"

***

Warrell nurses his ale before he speaks, downing it with slow sips and watching the lamplight flicker off the rows of dirty bottles behind the bar. It took some convincing on Myrrh's part, but Nab is back in Rikson's kitchen being watched over by the tavernkeep's wife. She'll talk to him later. Alone.

She keeps her dagger on the counter, hand resting on it while she takes small sips of her ale and waits. Earlier, she thought no one was watching, but now that her back's to the room, the whispers have started up. The piano isn't quite as loud as when she walked in. She wonders how much these people know about the events of late.

Warrell sets his empty mug down in a ring of foam that spilled over the top in the beginning. After inhaling deep through his nostrils, he starts to talk.

"It started a few days before"—he swallows—"before the Scythe marched into Rat Town and took Hawk. He came back after being gone for a week or two; do you remember?"

Myrrh nods. He'd been gone longer than usual that time. But it wasn't like they were family or anything, so when either she or Hawk vanished for a while, the other usually assumed they'd found lucrative work outside the district. Or at least that's what they told each other, though Nab had admitted to watching Hawk pace and grumble whenever she was away.

"Anyway, when he came back, he was madder than I'd ever seen him. Came stomping into this very tavern looking ready to breathe fire and burn the place down. I was honestly afraid to approach and waited till he'd doused some of that heat with a couple of ales."

Myrrh rotates her mug. She'd never seen Hawk angry like that—he certainly hadn't shown it when he came to their squat. It went against all his preaching about hiding emotions. But after what she's learned in the last couple weeks, he hid a lot more than his feelings from her.

"When I finally got up the courage to sit next to him, he seemed desperate to talk to someone. Said he'd been working on something, his biggest gig ever. He hoped to make life better for you and Nab, and all the grubbers for that matter. But he'd recently found out he'd been lied to."

Myrrh takes a deep swig of her ale, savors the bitterness on the back of her tongue before swallowing. "I know the feeling."

Warrell raises his eyebrows at this but says nothing. "Hawk wouldn't tell me any more. He was trying to figure out his revenge without getting you hurt it seems. He really cared about you, you know."

"I know," she says quietly. "I hate that he kept so much from me."

"I doubt you could have done anything to save him, if it's any consolation," Warrell says.

Myrrh shrugs.

"Finally, Hawk asked me to accompany him to meet with Slivers. Said he planned to hand them the best leverage they'd ever get against the Maire." Myrrh's ale is disappearing fast. She knows she should keep her head, but the thought of Hawk dealing with Glint's betrayal and never mentioning a thing to her...it eats at her. Brings back the grief of his loss all over again. Finally, she motions for the bartender who delivers a fresh mug.

"Did he tell you Glint is the Maire's son?" she asks, voice bitter.

Warrell glances at her sideways, perhaps in an attempt to commiserate. "Not beforehand. Slivers got the story out of him. Noble—he's the leader these days—"

"I know who Noble is."

"Sorry, Myrrh. You've been gone. Hard to remember what you were aware of."

She shakes her head. "Sorry for snapping. Fresh wounds, you know?"

He nods. "Hawk kept as much information as he could to himself, but Noble wouldn't commit to a deal without knowing what he was getting his syndicate into. So Hawk eventually coughed up the truth."

"I don't get why Slivers betrayed him. The opportunity to get their hands on the Maire's son seems priceless. What did Hawk want out of the deal?"

Behind them, a drunken argument quickly escalates to shouting, and Myrrh hears the smack of a fist contacting flesh. She can't bring herself to care right now. Just rotates her mug in her hands.

Warrell summons another drink and sucks off the foam. "That's the thing. All Hawk wanted was revenge. Didn't even ask for a finder's fee. Slivers swore up and down they had nothing to do with Hawk being taken. Truth is, there was almost a war down here over it. Grubbers versus the syndicate, and you know we wouldn't have won. They've got the numbers and the resources. Before it came to that though, Slivers discovered a snitch in their midst. Worked directly for the Maire."

Myrrh lets out a low whistle. "Ugly thing to uncover."

Warrell nods. "She's dead now."

"So the snitch told the Maire that someone was trying to sell out his son."

"Or they went straight to the Scythe. I suppose it doesn't matter how word got to her though."

Myrrh taps her heels against the barstool. Talk of the Scythe reminds her of Glint's claim that the woman has some bond oath to the family, enforced by old crag magic. She shakes her head. How did he do it? How did he lie so easily, pretending that all this information he had on the Maire came secondhand?

"Either way, as soon as the Scythe found out, she came for Hawk. Eliminated the threat to the Maire." And to his son, who she is probably *also* bound to defend.

Warrell nods. "The Scythe took him away just a couple days after we met with Noble."

Poor Hawk. Myrrh swallows, hard. At that moment, the hatred she feels toward Glint is as strong as any emotion she's experienced. Death isn't good enough for him.

"Which brings us to why I betrayed you," Warrell says. He waits until she meets his eyes. "I'm so sorry, Myrrh. It may not have been the best plan, but I thought it was our best chance to get revenge. I had to think fast when Glint's men approached me...maybe they really *did* think I sold Hawk out. I don't know. But I figured...I figured Glint wouldn't hurt you, not with your looks and skills, and if you truly believed I'd given you up, you'd"—Warrell's voice is thick with regret—"I figured Glint would find you intriguing enough that he'd trust you. I planned to make contact and get you out..."

"But?"

"I was expecting to deal with security hired by a high-society fop playing at banditry. Instead, I quickly discovered I'd mistakenly given you to a band of expert criminals. Your trail went cold within a few blocks of where they nabbed you. I'm so sorry."

She runs a hand through her hair. "Yeah, well, it's done. So, I see now why Slivers came after Glint. They're still planning to use him against his father. What about Nab? They took him and then decided to set him free?"

"Actually, they snatched the two boys out of respect for Hawk. Figured they'd be better off freed from Glint's organization."

"How did they find us—him? Glint's been secretive. Not trying to occupy turf like a regular syndicate."

"As it happens, my plan worked out. Just not in the way I imagined. After I lost you, I went to Slivers to ask for help. Or at least that they keep an eye out for you. Figured they'd be happy to assist if it might lead to Glint. One of their urchins saw you pass through Rat Town a few mornings ago."

Myrrh snorts. Ironic to think how safe she felt when coming through the district. She thought she'd passed through completely unnoticed.

"The kid followed you back, figured out where Glint was keeping you...after that, Slivers planned their operation and moved in hard."

"Do they still have him?"

Warrell nods. "They got in touch earlier this evening. Thought I'd want to know. Again, out of respect for Hawk."

"I want to see him."

"*If* they allow you access, you'll have to leave your weapons at the door. Don't get your hopes up about taking revenge."

"No, they caught him fair and square. Their score, their rules. I just want a chance to talk to him before they hand him over to his father...or whatever they plan to do. He needs to know that I figured him out. That he's nothing but filth to me now."

Chapter Twenty-Four

Myrrh steps into the room where Glint's being held. She's been stripped to her leathers and searched for weapons in ways that are decidedly inappropriate. None of that matters right now. Only the traitorous scum, tied to a chair and staring at her through eyelids swollen from a beating, is worth her attention.

He sucks a split lip when their eyes meet.

"So," he says. "You know."

"Which part, Glint? That you are the Maire's sixing son? Or that you're responsible for Hawk's death, and all this talk about revenge is just a big sixing lie? Do I know that the whole reason you've built up your gang is to protect your precious father? Yes, actually. I do know. I've recently discovered all those things and more." She shakes her head, voice trembling so much it's hard to speak. "I can't believe I trusted you. It makes me sick."

He looks down, struggling feebly against his bonds. "Myrrh..."

"Myrrh what? Are you still trying to find a new way to deceive me? You disgust me. I hope they decide you aren't worth trading to your father, because I know how mercy works with the Slivers. And I know that's my best hope for seeing you suffer for what you did."

She's pacing now, stalking back and forth across the small room heedless of the Slivers guard still standing in the doorway.

He turns his head to follow her. "Do you know how many times I wanted to tell you? Every time we joked about Rella and Merchant Giller, do you have any idea how it tore me up inside?"

"What a load of sixing pox!" she shouts. "I can't believe I..." She shakes her head. The attraction she felt for him is too disgusting to think about.

"I told Hawk the truth." He sits up straight, though she can see it's a struggle. "All along, I hated that he didn't know. Even though none of our early plans involved my father. Everything I told you about those days was true. We planned to build a..." His laugh is more of a sob. "I'll even call it a syndicate, seeing as this is likely the last chance I'll have to talk to you. Hawk and I wanted to do things a better way so that people like us—"

"Us?" Her voice is too shrill. Myrrh grits her teeth and forces her emotions back down. She can't let this man get to her that way.

"You're right. Not us. People like you and Hawk...all along, I was only pretending. But I did dream of creating an organization where we did better for people than my father does for the city. Criminal or not, I wanted lowborn citizens of Ostgard to have the chance to dream. But I was afraid that if Hawk knew the truth about my birth, he wouldn't want to work with me."

"So I'm supposed to feel sorry for you?"

"No, Myrrh. All I want is for you to know the truth before you condemn me. When I told Hawk, he disappeared. I guess my fears were justified. He couldn't bring himself to associate with the likes of me. I don't know what he did, but it must have been rash, because soon after, the Scythe came for him." He swallows. "I hope that sheds a little light on why I was afraid to let you in."

Myrrh can't believe he's still trying to manipulate her. She swallows back bile.

"Does it make you feel better to craft these lies? Do you come up with these explanations because a tiny part of you regrets what you've done?" She shakes her head. "I feel sorry for everyone who's dedicated the past months to you. I suppose I'll have to tell them before I leave town, because they're still sitting around Lower Fringe plotting your rescue."

"Hawk is alive." His words are so low she scarcely hears them. Stiffening, she glances at the door, but the Slivers guard has his head in the hallway listening to some shout elsewhere in the den.

A tiny, desperate part of her wants to believe him. Her eyes burn as tears threaten, and she blinks them fiercely away. How could he?

"It's true that I lied to you," Glint says in the same barely audible tone. "I will regret that for the rest of my life, however short that may be. The Maire is my father. But there's more to the story. If you won't listen for my sake, will you take the chance for Hawk? You can still walk out when I'm done talking. Slivers will still try to ransom me to my father, who will simply laugh and be glad I'm no longer around to embarrass him. Especially now that I failed in what he asked of me."

The words from the note spring to her mind. Something about a bargain between Glint and his father. She turns to him, fists clenched, eyes narrowed. For Hawk, she grits her teeth and nods. "Talk."

"I've been estranged from my father since the day of my mother's death," he says. "I stole her jewelry box and the contents of my father's safe and asked Bernard to help me secure passage down the Ost to the Port Cities. It was my father's scheming and plotting that got my beloved mother killed. All I had left of her was a locket with her image. And memories. Especially memories of her brutal death."

A tear falls from his swollen eye. Myrrh looks away so that his display of emotion won't soften her resolve.

"Bernard wouldn't let me go alone, the old fool. No one has told me..." He looks at her with such naked hope that she almost believes his concern. "Did he survive? Some of them came in through the kitchen when they took me."

"I don't know if you deserve that information," she says, her voice flat.

He looks away. "Maybe not. Maybe I will just have to hope. In any case, in the years after, I slowly worked my way up as a trader in the Port Cities. Until things changed there. I wasn't lying when I talked about how the rulers scrubbed the streets clean with the blood of the lower class. I realized then that it wasn't going to be enough for me to live outside my father's household. I needed to make a change, starting in the city where my mother died. So I came back about two years ago and started laying plans. That's when I met Hawk. And I'm telling the truth when I say that at first, I thought it shouldn't matter where I came from. It was only later when Hawk and I became close...I realized that I'd started to think of him as the father I never had. He deserved the truth." He shrugs. "You see how that turned out."

"It's a convincing tale," she says. "Much like everything else you told me."

"When Hawk left the safe house and didn't return, I hoped he just needed time to come to terms with working with someone like me. I was wrong, and I'm sorry."

Myrrh swallows. She doesn't want to meet his eyes right now. Doesn't want to let hope for Hawk grow.

Glint winces as he struggles against the cord binding his wrists. "I can't change that I deceived you, but thank you for giving me this chance to put it right. And I hope"—he leans and checks the guard at the door. The man is still distracted—"I hope you will consider what I'm going to tell you next," he says in a low, low voice. "I have no proof other than my word, but please believe me when I say I made a deal with my father. When I learned Hawk had been captured and by whom, I sent word asking for an audience. It was the first time I'd seen my father in nine years."

Myrrh's pace slows, because despite her best intents, she's starting to believe there's some truth in his words.

"My father knows that Emmerst and many in the council are plotting against him. That's another lie I told you. Another I'll never forgive myself for. Father also realized that I had a good chance of stopping the council from unseating him once I explained my ideas. He didn't care about the methods, only the results. The threat to his power must be removed. As a gesture of goodwill, he spared Hawk's life. Locked him in prison. But if Slivers hands me over, or worse, simply kills me, he'll do as he's threatened from the beginning. Hawk will die out of my father's spite."

At once, she believes him. She rushes the chair and gets in his face. "You had no right to keep that from me. If I'd known he was alive—"

"You would have what? Broken into my father's secret prison single-handedly? I don't even know where the sixing place is." Some of the fire returns to his voice as he stares back at her. "I never meant to keep the truth from you for so long. At first, I wasn't sure I could trust you with information about Hawk. Then I worried that if I told you and you ran off and got yourself killed, I'd have to carry that guilt for the rest of my life. And then, once I realized how selfish I was being, I was too afraid to admit the truth. Because we'd already gotten close, and I couldn't forget what had happened when I finally confessed to Hawk." He takes a deep breath. "I'm not asking for your forgiveness because I don't believe I deserve it. But I am asking you to believe me. At this point, maybe I deserve whatever Slivers does with me. But Hawk is innocent." He lowers his voice even more. "Help me get free, and we'll find a way to free Hawk. If you can't stomach keeping my bargain with my father, we can find another way."

He glances up over her shoulder and blinks swollen eyelids quickly. A sign for her to back away. She turns and sees the guard approaching.

"Stay away from the prisoner," he growls, grabbing her by the arm and dragging her out.

Myrrh looks over her shoulder at the battered man sitting alone in the bare room. Get him free? How in the sixing pox is she supposed to do that?

Chapter Twenty-Five

Myrrh crouches in the doorway of her old squat, the ramshackle stilt house in the Spills. On the muddy pathways below, late-working men and women return to their families. Heads down, navigating by the wan light of a half moon.

Hawk's bedroll is still here. She never had to decide to trade it to a rag seller for food or spare change. Hers and Nab's too, the blankets heaped against the walls. It's like their old grubber lives were just suspended all this time. Or maybe that their ghosts remained, going through the motions. Scrounging enough contracts to eat, always wondering if they should just give up and trade their freedom for the security of a syndicate membership.

Hawk is alive. If Glint's word isn't enough, she has proof in the crumpled letter he received from his father. Anger floods her veins when she thinks of how he kept it from her. But there's relief too. Hawk still has a chance.

But for how long? Without Glint, she has no way to get Hawk free. The Maire would sooner have her executed for knocking at his door than listen to her pleas. But Glint is a prisoner to one of the most ruthless gangs in the city. They tolerated her request to see him because she's been a trustworthy presence in Rat Town for years. Working the contracts Slivers won't bother with. Never treading on their business. Their charity will end the moment she works against their interests.

She needs to get him free despite the danger. Not because she cares what happens to him—she still hasn't made up her mind on that. Because he's the key to saving Hawk.

Unfortunately, she's not in much of a position to bargain. Even scrounging what she can from Glint's mansion, she'll never put together a ransom package worth considering. Glint's leadership is eager for a strike against Slivers, but they really don't have the resources. Not with Glint missing, the supply cache looted, and the situation with Porcelain Hand still unstable. Besides, after seeing where Glint's being held—deep within one of Slivers fortified dens—Myrrh's pretty sure he'd be dead by the time a rescue mission reached him. There's no chance of coming in quiet, and the Slivers guards will just kill him at the first sign of an attack.

Which means she needs a real plan. The kind of plot that Slivers *won't* expect. One of Hawk's lessons was that grubbers can't rely on the muscle of a syndicate to back them up. In other words, she'll gain nothing by brute force. She's got to use her head.

Myrrh retreats into the darkness of the squat. Leans against the wall. Closes her eyes and thinks.

***

Noble, the head honcho for the Slivers syndicate, stares at her from within a massive leather-upholstered armchair. He's balding, and the fringe of hair that encircles his head hangs well below his earlobes. Patchy scruff decorates his chin, and when he curls his lip in a snarl, yellowed teeth peek into view.

He doesn't invite her to sit, though three more chairs circle the animal-skin rug in the center of the room. She stops a pace short of treading on the dead thing's fur and runs eyes over the walls of Noble's den. The decor is nothing like the tasteful furnishings Glint was adding to his merchant's mansion—briefly, she wonders why his sense of taste didn't give her a clue that he wasn't being honest. Was she too lost in grief over Hawk? Too charmed by Glint's easy confidence? Either way, there's no question *this* room is home to a king among scoundrels. Gold and silver and mismatched art festoon the walls. And the whole place smells like liquor.

"You going to talk, or are you just wasting my time?" Noble holds a tumbler full of cloudy brown alcohol in yellowed fingers thick with calluses.

"I've come to beg for Hawk's life," she says, chin raised.

"Sixing waste of time. I knew it." He sighs heavily. "Little rat's gone mad over losing her daddy. Hawk's dead, girl."

She shakes her head. "The Scythe took him. Enough people saw it; there's no question. But after that, everyone just assumed she killed him like she has every other thief she's captured. She didn't. He's alive."

"And you know this because?"

"Because Glint convinced his father to spare Hawk's life. And the minute you execute him, Hawk dies."

Noble takes a sip from his drink, then rests the tumbler over his crotch. "Glint told you this? *Surely* there's no ulterior motive there..."

"I have proof." She starts to pull out the crumpled letter.

"Frankly, I don't care if you do."

She blinks. "But...Hawk's life depends on it."

"It's a sad tale. Tragic. Another lowlife grubber ground down beneath the heel of the Maire's regime." He raises his glass in a mock toast to a lost friend.

Keep it together, Myrrh.

"You know the Maire won't ransom Glint."

"I don't know that for sure." He shifts his bulk in his seat. "And to be frank, I'm sort of hoping he doesn't. It will give me the excuse to do exactly as I please with the fruit of the Maire's sixing loins. Humiliation. Execution. How many people like me get this kind of chance?"

Her nostrils flare. "In that case, as I said, I came to bargain. Perhaps I can offer you something more enticing than the chance to beat a man to death."

"Actually, you said you came to beg."

"Allow me to correct myself then. I'd like to make a deal."

The man's cheek twitches. "Could it be you've taken a fancy to the highborn lad?" He hawks and spits the goblin mucus onto his rug. "No deal."

"This isn't about Glint. Hawk did good work for the people of Rat Town. You know that."

"And I'm sorry he suffered the fate most of your ilk will eventually face. A hard life and an anonymous death—or, if you prefer to cling to your delusions, a last few years spent rotting in a dank prison cell."

"You aren't sorry, or you'd listen to my offer."

He laughs without mirth. "You got me. What's the life of a poor grubber compared to my chance to hit the Maire where it hurts?"

Myrrh focuses on Hawk's lessons. Her emotions remain locked deep down under her heart and lungs where this worthless piece of trash can't see them. She's all business when she fixes him with a hard stare.

"I can give you and your best men a full night's looting access to the Maire's palace. You won't run into any trouble. Take whatever you want."

He taps his fat finger on his glass. "I'm listening."

Chapter Twenty-Six

Three nights later, Myrrh and a collection of thieves huddle near the exit for the storm drain that tunnels beneath Maire's Quarter. As the barge they crossed to reach the drain moves out of the passage beneath the bridge, Mink flashes the vessel's spotter with a quick blink of gratitude from their hooded lantern. The spotter raises his lamp in acknowledgment as the barge moves on up the river, burly men working their poles in the same cadence they've kept since the vessel came into view.

They're committed now.

Myrrh peers over the dark water and makes eye contact with Resh. The big man stands against the previous pillar, having accompanied them this far to impress upon the Slivers gang members the new ownership of this particular thieves' path. The man meets her stare and gives a solemn nod. As soon as he returns to Lower Fringe, he and the remnants of Porcelain Hand will begin their part of the plot.

Myrrh feels a moment of doubt, wondering if she can count on the members of the rival syndicate, especially so soon after Glint moved against them. But given the rewards they've been offered, she suspects they'll attack the task with enthusiasm.

She turns back toward the group crowding the end of the tunnel. All told, there are seven members of Slivers, hand chosen by Noble for this chance at the best pickings in town. Glint and Mink stand apart from the Rat Town thieves, clear in their distrust of the Rat Towners. At Myrrh's nod, Mink passes packets of glimmer to the Slivers thieves, part of the bargain Myrrh negotiated. She then steps back to the tunnel exit to stash the lantern for later.

When the eyes of the Slivers thugs gleam silver in the darkness, Myrrh leads the band forward. They stop at the exit for the storm drain, ears cocked for noise in the alley above. This time of night, merchants and their consorts are returning from dinner parties and cocktails, and false laughter bubbles over the street. But the sounds are distant. The alley seems deserted.

Myrrh nods and opens her canvas sack. Unlike Glint, who could make his way across the barges in formal dining attire, she wasn't about to try to balance on a plank bridge above sewage and then leap from ship to ship in a ridiculous dress. Not when she hopes to arrive wearing something other than awful-smelling tatters. She pulls out the gray-velvet gown that Lavi purchased all those days ago.

The others wait expectantly. Myrrh rolls her eyes and raises an eyebrow at the men until they turn their backs. She slips out of her leathers and slides the gown over her head.

"Okay," she says. As they turn around, she puts her back in front of Glint. He fastens the buttons with none of the teasing fingers and loaded words from before. She's made it clear that she doesn't know what to think of him, and he seems smart enough not to try flirting.

Once the dress is secured, she pulls out her jade necklace, clasps it around her neck.

Glint looks away, an unreadable expression on his face. Or maybe not so unreadable. She has no doubt he regrets what he did.

"Which one of you comes with us?" she asks Noble. The ugly man leans against the wall, looking surly, as he nudges one of his thieves in the back of the knee. The spindly man steps forward, smoothing hair that may have been brushed tonight for the first time in years. He almost looks respectable.

Almost.

With the Queen of Nine's blessing, the shock of their arrival will distract from his appearance. Having a Slivers member along throughout the night was part of Noble's requirements for the deal. If he was going to release Glint, he needed to be sure it wasn't just an elaborate escape plot. The thief will pose as an added security guard, but he'll carry a set of poison darts somewhere on his body. Myrrh doesn't doubt he'd use them if Glint tried to run.

"We'll notify you when it's time," she says.

Noble curls his lip. "Fine."

Mink slips into the alley first, scanning the surroundings before motioning Glint and Myrrh up from the dark. The Slivers man follows, eyes wide at the experience of stepping onto a Maire's Quarter street. After Myrrh crouches to lower the grate into place, Glint leads the group onto a wider street and toward the palace.

"He won't budge on the agreement," he says, stepping close to Myrrh. "Not to mention, I assume you understand the dangers of bringing thugs into the Quarter."

She's kept him ignorant of the plan on purpose. Better that he doesn't know some of her contingencies. But clearly, he's not used to having someone else in charge. "And those are?"

"There's a reason it's easy to walk openly here. Would-be thieves must use caution if we don't wish to lose the privilege in the future."

"No one will know they've been here."

He sticks his hands in his pockets, reminding her of their leisurely night strolls. "I don't think they're here to sightsee."

"No, they're not. But do you remember that trust we built? The trust you betrayed, I should add?"

His jaw clenches. Myrrh looks away to keep from getting distracted. Even beneath the swelling on his face, the fading bruises and cuts that mar his cheekbones, his features are striking.

"Fair enough. As long as you've considered that I might have useful input as far as your plan goes."

"I have. Listen, Glint, I respect your opinion. I'm even on my way to forgiving you. But it's just better this way. The more you question things, the harder it is for me to focus."

"I'll just have to trust you then." He turns down another street, winding his way through the district with easy familiarity. And why not? His father might not have been the Maire when Glint still lived with him, but if the family didn't have a house in Maire's Quarter, they surely had plenty of invitations to dinners and such.

After another few blocks of walking, Glint's pace slows. He stops near a semicircular staircase of white stone and nods, face a mix of disdain and uncertainty. Clearly, they've arrived.

Atop the stairs, double doors stand closed. Carved of dark wood and inset with some sort of green stone, they are as formidable as the army of Shields that guards the district.

Myrrh swallows and ascends the marble stairs. She knocks before she loses her nerve.

An annoyed expression twists the servant's face when he opens the door. "Yes?"

"We've come to see the Maire."

Annoyance fades to disdain as the servant looks them up and down. He curls his lip in disgust at the sight of Glint's injured face. "Audiences are by appointment only. Good night."

He tries to shut the door, but Myrrh shoves a tightly laced boot into the gap. Even with the protection of the leather, she grunts in pain as the heavy corner smashes her foot.

"Actually, you'll want to go check with him. Tell him his son and fiancée have come to call."

The servant blinks. Glint coughs in surprise but quickly covers it. He steps forward and suddenly transforms from a regretful thief to the commanding son of the most powerful man in the city.

"Go ask," he says. "We'll wait."

The servant thins his lips and glances down at Myrrh's foot. She withdraws it from the gap, and the door clicks shut. Footsteps retreat into the house.

Shortly, the door swings open again.

"The Maire will see you as soon as he has changed out of his nightclothes. Might I offer you a late dinner?"

"Please," Myrrh says as she sweeps into the foyer.

***

The wine has been poured and the table set for three by the time the Maire stalks into the room. Myrrh sees where Glint inherited his looks. The man is handsome, nearly to a fault. His dark hair sets off his keen eyes and straight nose, his pair of lips that curve just right. But where Glint wears those same features with confidence, his father has twisted them into a cruel arrogance.

Under Glint's gaze, Myrrh often felt as if she were being judged. Held up to a standard in Glint's mind.

His father immediately discards her as trash.

"Let me guess," the Maire says as he circles the table like a predator. "You found a nice girl. Managed to impress her with the modest results of your trading business in the Port Cities. Or did you woo her with your criminal takings?"

Glint takes a deep breath and raises his wine glass for a swallow.

"Or, wait"—the man rounds the table until he stands behind Glint, facing her—"you *did* tell her you're an unrepentant rogue now, didn't you? What do you think of that, Miss..." He scans her up and down as if wondering where his son found such a gutter scamp.

"Miss Aventile," she says with a clipped voice. "And we met under circumstances that have nothing to do with my fiancé's business dealings—"

The Maire laughs. "Lies. I know exactly how women think. And they *always* have their eyes on the treasure they'll gain by opening their legs."

Glint sets his glass down so hard wine splashes over the rim. At the far end of the room, a pair of the Scythe's underlings stiffens as their hands twitch toward their weapons. In the antechamber beyond, Mink rises from a richly upholstered sofa and nears the doorway in three liquid strides.

Myrrh glances the other direction, toward the wall behind the head of the table. The Scythe is a statue in her red leathers, moving nothing but her eyes as she follows her master's movements. Myrrh has no doubt she calculated Glint's intent the moment he slammed his glass down, deciding it was an expression of anger, not a threat to the Maire.

"Don't tell me this is the first time you've learned the shallow truth behind a woman's interest...what do you go by now? Glint?"

"Your *son*," Myrrh says, stressing the word, "does not need to fear such motives with me."

"Unlike his mother?" the Maire says, eyes cruel as he watches Glint's shoulders hunch.

Despite Glint's betrayal, Myrrh feels nothing for him right now but pity. How must it have been to grow up with this sixing pig for a father?

Glint inhales, releasing the stem of his glass and turning a hateful glare to his father. "Nothing you've ever done—no wealth, no Maire's title—*nothing* has made you worthy of Mother's affection. If her father hadn't forced her into the marriage, she *never* would have chosen someone like you."

The Maire stalks to a side door and kicks it. "Where is our dinner service?" he shouts before returning to sit at the head of the table.

Silence gathers for a moment until a servant sticks her head out the door. "First course in less than five minutes, Maire."

The Maire's napkin snaps in the air as he shakes out the folds and lays it in his lap. "Of course, the worst part of my marriage is that I ended up with you. Isn't that ironic? What happened to your face, by the way? Lose another fight?"

During the exchange, Myrrh's gaze flicks to the Scythe. The woman's face remains still, untouched by emotion. Except for the little twitch of anger in her lower eyelid. And *something* deep in her eyes.

"As I was saying, I met Glint under surprising circumstances," Myrrh says as if the other conversation isn't happening. "I was looking for my father."

"And you came to my no-good son looking for help?" The Maire laughs. "What terrible luck for you."

This time, the Scythe blinks when the Maire explicitly acknowledges his relationship to Glint.

"Not exactly. My da went missing, you see. After paying a visit to Rat Town, of all places. We're traders from upriver trying to expand into Ostgard, and I hate to say, but my father had a bad habit of looking for deals where other people of breeding are afraid to tread."

"Now I get it," the Maire says, sneering at Glint. "You swindled this girl's father. He got wise to it and took out his lost earnings on your face." His brows draw together. "No. That's not right. Surely the girl didn't fall for you with your face in that condition, especially if her father's responsible. Maybe *she* knocked you around when she learned you were my son. Realized what a fortune she was missing out on, so whacked you in the face until you agreed to come beg for your inheritance."

"His name is Hawk," Myrrh says. "My father."

The smile drops from the Maire's face.

Before the conversation can continue, a trio of servants emerges from the kitchen. Balanced on their hands, three bowls of soup steam. They smell delicious. Briny in a way Myrrh doesn't recognize. Nonetheless, she ignores the offering and keeps her gaze on the Maire. And the Scythe behind him.

"I'm sure it is," the Maire says.

"Is what?"

"His name. Hawk. Do you speak often? Because you seem to have a problem with clarity."

The Maire lifts a spoonful of the creamy soup, blows on it, and tips it past his lips. Across the table from her, Glint grabs his spoon in a white-knuckled grip. His nostrils flare as he sucks angry breaths into his lungs. Myrrh extends her leg under the table and touches his shin with her foot. He jumps, catches her eyes, then makes a visible effort to relax.

Myrrh takes a bite of her soup to help him along. The taste is divine, bursting with herbs and garlic and some kind of springy meat.

"So this is where the story gets really interesting," she says. "It had been three days since my father left our guesthouse in West Fifth, and I couldn't stand it anymore. I took my personal bodyguard"—she waves at Mink in the antechamber—"and went down to Rat Town to find him. As you can imagine, I was shocked by the squalor, but people there were so helpful. Half a day later, I was knocking on Glint's door. And it turns out, he and my father had been talking about going into business together."

The Maire rolls his eyes. "Wonder of wonder. And did you have any notion what kind of *business* this was? I believe I recently mentioned my son's criminal enterprises."

"Oh, well, my father was known to...hmm...get creative with his methods. But only when it would truly benefit people in need. And from what I've learned in the days since Glint promised to help me locate my da, your son shares the same altruism. I feel so fortunate. And frankly, besotted."

She turns a cloying smile on Glint, trying to drag him out of his funk with the ridiculous act. He doesn't look up from his soup.

"Ah," the Maire says, spooning another bite of soup into his mouth. "But you see, in Ostgard, we don't allow *creativity* in business methods. The city depends on the tariffs we impose and those who work outside the system only *harm* the poor workers."

"But that's just it!" Myrrh says. "It works so much better when the benefits go directly to the people who work so hard for them. That's what Da always says, and he runs his businesses according to those principles. Back home, the people love him. They run out of their houses when his barges come to the docks. Once your son and I are married, I can't wait to bring him home and show him off."

Maybe she's overdoing it, but the Scythe is getting more and more interested.

The Maire sneers at Glint. "So you're planning to rescue the damsel by freeing her father. How's that going?"

"Actually," Glint says, sitting up straight, "I thought you might have an idea where we might find him. The Shield Watch does report to you, right? They wouldn't imprison a man without trying him for his crimes, would they?"

Glint glares at his father.

His father smiles back.

"Wait! That's right!" Myrrh turns wide eyes to the Maire. "You would know if anything terrible happened to my father, right? His name is Hawk."

"We had a deal, father," Glint says in a low voice.

"And I'm keeping my end of it."

"How do I know that?" Glint's soup splashes when he drops his spoon into the bowl. "Why should I do your dirty work without seeing proof you can uphold your end of the bargain?"

The Maire's eyes narrow. "It's proof you want? Care to escort your darling—and vapid headed—fiancée to Craghold? I think she'd find it interesting to learn what our city does to smugglers and crooks. Seeing as she wants to marry one."

"Craghold, huh? It sounds like you've done great things with our ancestral home."

"It's secure and beyond the reach of my...adversaries. I find it quite useful as a place to store important things."

"What are you guys talking about?" Myrrh asks, looking from one to the other. Craghold. So the Maire has converted their ancestral home into his private prison? She planned to bait the conversation until he gave up enough information for her to find Hawk. Has she succeeded?

She fixes her gaze on Glint, willing him to confirm. With the faintest nod, he speaks. "It's nothing, darling. Just my father blustering about the home we left so that he could grow our fortune in Ostgard. He assumes you'd be aghast at the mountain weather. But I know you're hardier than that, right?"

She looks down as if embarrassed by the praise. "If I were with you, it wouldn't matter where we lived. We'd have to bring Da, of course."

"Isn't this adorable?" The Maire rolls his eyes.

Myrrh hikes up her dress to reach the thigh holster where she sheathed her dagger. She glances into the antechamber and catches Mink's gaze. The assassin watches as Myrrh picks up her wine glass, takes two sips in quick sequence, and sets it back down. That's the signal. Mink springs, knives flashing. Within heartbeats, she has a blade at the throat of one of the Scythe's underlings. The other's arm is pinned to the wood paneling, a long knife stuck through the wrist and out the other side. Blood spurts from the wound.

Myrrh jumps and knocks the Maire's chair over backward. She falls down after him and lands with a knee on the man's chest, her dagger at his throat.

"No!"

Relief spreads through her when Glint shouts. He's fast. She knows how fast. An eyeblink later, his weight falls across her, shielding her from the Scythe's quickly drawn sword.

The Scythe is loyal to the Maire's family line. But not to the Maire himself, necessarily. To the family, as vowed under the old oaths of the crags. All these years, she's faithfully executed the Maire's commands, imprisoning and killing innocent people because her unbreakable oaths demanded it. During this time, she's believed Glint to be dead or vanished. But tonight, the conversation has proved without a doubt that the Maire's son is alive. More, he's chosen a would-be bride to continue the family name.

She can't strike Glint. And with the right convincing, it will be obvious she can't strike Myrrh either. Not the future mother of her next oathlord.

Glint rolls slowly, jabbing Myrrh with elbows and knees as he does everything he can to defend her with his body. Beneath her, the Maire groans and feebly calls for help.

"Take command," Myrrh whispers. "She's yours by oath."

"What?"

Myrrh speaks louder so the Scythe can hear. "Her oath is to the family line, not a single individual. You are the future of your household. More, you'll never demand the cruelties your father has. She can choose you without breaking her vows."

She feels muscles tighten in his back as he understands her plan. Slowly, his arms drop, still shielding her, but no longer upheld in defense.

"Tell your men they are not to attack us," he says in a level voice.

"Dob. Relenz. Stand down." The Scythe's voice is full of more than command. Her tone practically drips with relief over being released from the Maire's cruel rule.

Myrrh removes her dagger from the man's throat. She was ready to kill him tonight to ensure that Glint was the only remaining heir to the family line. But it won't be necessary.

Chapter Twenty-Seven

The Maire shouts through his gag—one of his expensive linen napkins—as Mink grins and scratches his neck with the tip of one of her knives. A drop of blood runs down to his collar. Almost immediately, his pupils dilate, and he goes limp but not completely unconscious. Susceptible to commands, able to stagger forward while supported by someone lending a shoulder.

The effects of the very light dose of nightbark coating Mink's blade.

Myrrh steps into the kitchen as Mink unfastens the gag. The servants look up in alarm, sure that their master has come to punish them for some inadequacy in the meal.

"Missus?" says the servant who opened the front door. Remembering the disdain on his face when he first looked at her, Myrrh is tempted to say nothing. Let him be surprised when a band of hardened criminals arrives to ransack the place. But that's just petty.

"You should leave the premises. All of you. It won't be safe here in half an hour."

"The Maire would not—"

"I'm not going to waste time convincing you. We're taking the Maire with us. Feel free to watch us go."

She spins on her heels and hurries back into the dining room. Mink and Glint have the Maire on his feet, his arms slung over their shoulders. He looks like a stumbling drunk. Steely gaze firm, the Scythe nods. Her presence will be enough to discourage questions.

"Your associates will arrive soon," Myrrh says to the Slivers thief as they exit the front door. "Finish your work, and be out of the district an hour before dawn."

He nods and shuts the door behind them, and then they're alone in the streets, a small group of concerned family escorting the Maire somewhere he can sober up beyond the judging eyes of the city council. The Scythe trails behind with one of her underlings. The other, the man who suffered Mink's knife through the wrist, disappeared at the Scythe's command. Likely sent to bandage his wound and pass the word to the other blades in service to the Scythe. Their allegiance has changed.

Near the alley where they entered the district, Glint shifts the burden of his father onto Mink and steps toward Myrrh.

"Impressively done," he says as he looks down at her. He's standing close enough she can smell the sandalwood that seems to cling to his skin even after his days of imprisonment.

She swallows and shifts back. A flash of sadness crosses his face.

"What are your plans for him?" he asks in a low voice. "I have no love for the man. Quite the opposite. But..."

But it's difficult with family. So she's heard. Myrrh doesn't remember her parents.

"I was prepared to kill him if necessary," she says. "I won't lie about that. Hawk's life is worth twenty of his."

"But you won't."

She shakes her head.

His shoulders sag in what looks like a mix of relief and disappointment.

At the storm drain, Myrrh crouches and hisses to the waiting Slivers men. Noble swings the grate open and clambers—agile despite his stocky build and advancing years—onto the street. His eyes widen at the sight of their captive. Myrrh might not have seen the Maire in person before tonight, but clearly the Slivers kingpin has.

"Help us get him down, and you're free to take your pickings," she says.

With a nod, he whispers low commands to his thieves. Moments later, the Maire is slumped in a heap against the tunnel wall, and the Slivers gang is skulking in the alley, peering nervously toward the well-lit street ahead.

Myrrh stands facing Noble, her feet planted and arms crossed. "Move through the streets alone or in pairs. Walk with purpose, and no one will bother you. Be gone from the district an hour before dawn."

"And be discreet," Mink adds, "or you'll ruin opportunities for every sixing thief in the city."

Noble nods.

"We square then?" Myrrh asks. "Glint's free to go, and you have your loot."

"Square," he says.

With a nod, Myrrh climbs down the ladder. The looting will keep Noble busy for at least another few hours. Plenty of time to finish out her plan.

***

At the tunnel mouth, Mink grabs the hooded lantern and starts flashing a signal. On the next island, a hunched figure picks up the command and passes it to the next pillar. More low-level members of Glint's organization will pass the word from there.

Myrrh bounces on her toes, fingers absently working the sign of the Queen of Nines, until she spots the light from a barge sweeping around the first downstream turn where the river starts its S curve around Maire's Quarter and the Neck. She holds her breath as the shout travels over the water, the command for the oarsmen to paddle backward. The barge slows as it approaches the bridge. In the bow, her newly hired spotter, a down-on-her-luck smuggler from Carp's Refuge, raises the lantern high and calls directions to the man at the tiller. The central openings in the bridge are easier for downstream traffic to navigate through, but Myrrh didn't want to attempt to bring the Maire across any of the gaps.

She winces when the nose of the barge grazes the retaining wall, but a quick correction on the part of the tillerman rights the barge and slides it into the gap. The vessel is moving too fast for conversation as the spotter passes. Myrrh settles for a nod of approval. When the center of the barge is directly below the exit to the storm drain, Mink laughs and throws the Maire down onto the deck. He lands in a heap, oblivious to his surroundings. Myrrh smirks when she imagines his reaction once the nightbark wears off. By then, her bargemen will have the man restrained and imprisoned in the cabin.

It's a long journey down the Ost, onto the wide sea beyond the Port Cities, and along a sheltered course of island hopping to a particular debtor's colony near the Hevish Archipelago. She's learned a lot of geography over the past few days of planning this operation. It should be an interesting journey for a man who's known nothing but obedience all his life.

Her new bargemen will need to exercise self-restraint to avoid harming the man who imposed the tariffs that kept them in abject poverty all these years. But she thinks they're up to the task. Especially now that she's offering them eighty percent of the profits from future trade. The recently refitted barge is currently loaded with Inner Kingdom goods. She bartered them from Jak in exchange for the rest of the spice haul. This first cargo won't make her new crew rich, but it's a start, and with the coin they earn, they'll be able to stack the decks for a return journey.

It's the beginning of her smuggling empire, just one of the things she has planned for her future.

With the Maire taken care of, Myrrh steps back and shakes Mink's hand. So far so good. Now to wait for vessels to get them out of Maire's Quarter. Glint's people should have already started moving toward Rat Town, but she hopes to make it there in time to catch at least *some* of the action.

Chapter Twenty-Eight

Unfortunately, Glint's people are too fast. By the time she strides into Rat Town, velvet dress dragging in the mud and followed by a bewildered Glint, there's a trail of Slivers thieves sprawled in the streets. Most are still alive, clutching their heads as they regain consciousness or wrapping bandages around sliced-up limbs. When they spot Glint, they raise hands in additional surrender.

The taverns and gambling dens that served as bases of operations for the Slivers syndicate now blaze with light. Like exterminators evicting vermin, Glint's people throw anyone who argues out into the street. Guards with arms the size of ships' masts now stand over the entrances.

After a few blocks spent shuffling forward and gawking, Glint finally stops in his tracks.

"How?"

She shrugs. "It was *your* plan."

His brow furrows. "What do you mean?"

From a long pocket stitched against her rib cage, she pulls out the paper with his notes on the Slivers dens and defenses. Glint steps under a lantern to read.

He swallows.

"Yes, it was in your locked drawer."

"Then you found the letter from my father. That's how you put things together."

"And the locket with a picture of your mother. I thought it was a girlfriend you hadn't mentioned."

He chews his lip and looks down. "I don't want to think about how you felt when finding this stuff."

"Angry. Betrayed. Fortunately, I got a chance to vent already, back when you were tied to a chair."

"I"—he shakes his head—"what's the use of another apology? I can't even forgive myself. Anyway, you used my notes to organize a strike. But Slivers is a massive syndicate. Too big for us to take on." He watches another Slivers thief get shoved out onto the street. "Or so I thought."

"The Slivers syndicate is no different than your organization. Without leadership, the underlings just aren't capable of organizing."

His eyes widen with sudden understanding. "And their leaders are currently picking through my father's possessions. Oblivious to what's going on here."

"Exactly."

"What happens when they return? We don't have the resources to hold both Rat Town and Lower Fringe. I assume the situation with the recruits from Porcelain Hand is tense, at best."

"They won't return, at least not with any ability to lead."

A brief flash of guilt tightens Myrrh's chest until she remembers the things Noble said about grubbers. He was willing to trade Hawk's life for the mere chance to punish Glint for a birth he didn't choose. Noble's inner circle is no better. She's worked in Rat Town long enough to know that.

"Explain."

"Noble was insistent that I supply his team with glimmer. Rumors about the advantages it's been giving your organization have spread, it seems."

The guilt must be clear in her voice because Glint touches her arm. He jerks his hand away when she stiffens. The gentle smile that had teased the corners of his mouth vanishes. Myrrh has to look away to keep from reacting. Until Hawk is free, emotions are just a distraction.

"Sorry," she says. "Jumpy tonight."

"And you still aren't ready to forgive me."

"I'm working on it."

"So the glimmer...you changed the dose?"

She nods. "Four times what we use. That should be enough, I assume."

He glances toward the eastern sky. A few hours until dawn still. "I imagine so. When the sun rises, they'll be glimmer-blind."

"Whites, as you called them, right?"

"Unable to handle sunlight without extreme pain. Even lanterns will be difficult. You made some powerful enemies today, Myrrh. I wonder if I should send people to ambush them on the way out of Maire's Quarter."

"Don't. I made a bargain. I'll keep my word. They're free to go with whatever they stole from your father's palace."

Glint sighs and looks up at the torchlit haze that now hangs over the city. "I won't try to convince you."

"Good."

They keep walking. Around them, Rat Town is strangely silent. Reeling from the upheaval. Myrrh turns down an alley leading to Rikson's Roost.

"Even without the Slivers bigwigs, I'm still not sure we can hold both districts," Glint says after a while.

"No. The situation with Porcelain Hand is shaky enough."

"How did you convince them to support this operation?"

"Same way a savvy person convinces a thief of anything. I appealed to their greed. An even split of the proceeds from gutting the Slivers coffers."

"So even if Slivers tries to reorganize, they won't have the resources to fund the recovery."

"Exactly."

"That leaves something of a...void in the criminal fabric of the city."

"Maybe not," she says, looking aside so he can't read her expression.

"What do you mean?"

"You'll see. Anyway, the changes in Rat Town won't be any more dramatic than what Maire's Quarter will wake up to," she says.

Glint snorts. "Good point."

"Is Merchant Emmerst really the threat you claimed? Will he gain control of the council and the Maire's title?"

Glint chews his lip, thinking. "Hmm. Yes to the first question. Regardless of the lies I told you, I also did my best to lace them with as much truth as I could. Emmerst can't be allowed to take control, or every honest thief in the city will find themselves out of work. That wouldn't be so bad if lawful jobs were added to replace the lost opportunities." He shakes his head. "As if that would happen here."

He stops walking and nudges a stone embedded in the muddy street, prying at it with his toe until he can kick it free.

"You didn't answer my second question."

"Because I don't want to make a commitment I can't keep. I will do everything I can to stop Emmerst's play for power. But it won't be easy. Someone else will need to attract council support and the title nomination."

She turns to face him. "Merchant Giller, you mean?"

He shrugs. "Maybe I can find another merchant to rally the council around. Either way, it's going to be a challenge." Glint glances up and casts her a bittersweet smile. "I don't imagine Rella wants to help?"

Myrrh swallows the traitorous heat that rises toward her cheeks. "I won't be able to join you."

The faint flare of hope in his eyes fades. "I understand."

"For starters, I set out for Craghold tomorrow. I was wondering...I'm sure I *can* break in and free the prisoners, but a little help wouldn't hurt my chances."

He nods, back to business. "I'll send the Scythe with you. Her word alone will open the prison gates. You'll be back within a fortnight."

Myrrh continues forward, and he hurries to catch up.

"As for afterward," he says, "my leaders followed you tonight...I think we could make an announcement of your formal promotion. Just like we planned."

She doesn't respond. Not until they reach the stoop of Rikson's Roost. She stops in the square of light near the open door and takes a deep breath. She knew he'd ask her about stepping up as a leader in his organization if the plot tonight succeeded. And she's already decided her answer. She just didn't expect to find it so hard to cough out the words.

"Come inside," she says. "I think we've earned a drink. We can talk about the future later."

***

A cheer goes up when she steps into the room. Myrrh scans the gathered faces and smiles.

Against the wall, around two dozen Slivers members have been bound and gagged. She'll have to release them eventually, but not until she talks to them about their future prospects in Rat Town. A few might be redeemable. Allowed to stay on as grubbers or low-level lackeys. The rest can find their way to another district. Or better, another city.

Standing guard over the captives, Warrell gives her a solemn nod. She returns the gesture and threads her way through tables to take a seat at the bar.

Nab, head pillowed on his arms, is snoring lightly. Beside him, Tep nurses a watered-down ale. He's practicing a flinty stare in the mirror and jumps when he realizes she's caught him at it.

"Stick to cooking," she says. "Bernard will work himself to death if you aren't there to help."

The boy glares. Myrrh looks away before she succumbs to the urge to tease him more. As she climbs onto the stool beside Nab, the boy jerks awake, mumbling something unintelligible. He quickly shakes his head to clear it and swipes a hand toward his mug.

"Have a nice nap?" she asks.

"I wasn't sleeping," he says, tongue still slow.

"Right."

The boy blinks again, clearing the last of the fog. His eyes narrow when he spots Glint.

When Myrrh visited during the days she was putting the operation together, she explained the truth about Glint's past. Given how Nab idolized him, she expected him to forgive the man. But Nab, apparently, has other ideas.

"Have you kept up with your reading over the past days?" Glint asks, ignoring the boy's expression.

"How dare you lie to her?" Nab spits. "Myrrh deserves better. Even the lowliest grubber in the Spills is better than some rich heir pretending to be a thief just to charm her off her feet."

"It's okay, Nab," she says gently. "Glint is well aware how much he screwed up by lying to me."

"Yeah, well, I'm not sure you know what's good for you anymore. You're still hanging out with him, aren't you?"

"But not in that way," Glint says. He looks down at the bar top. "There never was a *that* way to be honest."

Nab angrily sucks down a deep swallow of ale. Myrrh shakes her head. She's going to have to talk with Rikson about serving alcohol to the kid.

"And now you're just going to move back into his mansion," Nab says. "Pretend everything's fine?"

"No, Nab. I'm not. Tomorrow, I'm going to go get Hawk. And after that..." She glances back toward Warrell and the captives. "We have work to do around Rat Town, right?"

He turns wide eyes her way. "We're staying?"

"For now."

Beside her, Myrrh feels Glint sinking over the bar top. He raises a hand in a lackluster gesture to order an ale from the woman working the taps. Myrrh sighs. Maybe she should have found the courage to tell him her plans *before* they entered the room.

"Back to the squat?" Only a hint of dismay enters Nab's voice.

"Actually, I believe there are a number of Slivers safe houses that are now empty of occupants. Maybe we could appropriate one of those."

Nab tries to keep his cool, but he can't help tapping his dangling feet against the barstool in excitement. "I get to pick my room?"

"And the room where your tutor will meet you for reading lessons."

Glint gives an amused huff as Nab sputters. Myrrh resists the urge to lay a hand on the man's knee. This parting of ways is much harder than she expected.

"If I don't have to pretend to be his little brother anymore, why do I gotta learn that sixing stuff?"

"Hey!" Myrrh snaps. "Language..."

Nab rolls his eyes.

"Anyway, you have to be able to read because that is a requirement of all members of the Ghost syndicate."

"Wait, what?" Glint says.

Myrrh spins on her stool and motions for Warrell. "You mentioned a void in the criminal fabric. I agree that's a problem. It could lead to a turf war during an otherwise golden opportunity for thievery in Ostgard. While the merchants scramble for influence and plot against each other to decide the next Maire, they'll have a harder time defending against pilferers and knaves."

He shakes his head as if desperately confused. "You're founding a new syndicate?"

Myrrh swallows, forcing away the impulse to soften the news. She knows he wants more from her, both personally and professionally.

"Yes, Mistress?" Warrell asks as he steps up to join the conversation.

"Any word from the strike teams? Problems?"

"Smooth as silk. They're moving in to take possession of the hideouts as Glint's people retreat with their spoils."

"But where are you getting the resources?" Glint asks. "You didn't flip the loyalty of the Slivers organization that easily, did you?"

"Some of them will flip, I imagine. But that's the thing about Rat Town. Freelancers work solo or in pairs, so you never really get a gist of how many of us there are, but we have at least as many grubbers as syndicate members running jobs down here. We're an independent sort."

"Independent, but not stupid," Warrell says. "Mistress Myrrh promised changes for Rat Town. Big ones."

Glint blinks. "So you organized those who refuse to be led and somehow made them swear fealty anyway."

"For now, the questions of leadership will be rather more fluid than that. We'll have a council of thieves. A process for organizing our operations that involves everyone. Even if we weren't a syndicate of freelancers, I don't have a choice on that. I'll be gone for the first fortnight of our reign over Rat Town. And I won't make the same mistake as you and every kingpin in the city."

"Leaving an organization helpless when the leader isn't around to issue orders," Glint says.

"Exactly."

Myrrh leans back and props her elbows on the bar. She surveys the room, the new members of Ghost sketching plans on the tabletops by dragging fingers through trails of moisture from their ales. A young woman taps out a tune on the piano, humming along. As far as the founding moments of an empire go, it's been a good night.

"Well," Glint says, "given what your man here reports, my people are already on their way back to Lower Fringe. I suppose I should get back to start putting things back together. See what I can do about bringing Porcelain Hand into the organization."

"Your gang really needs a name," Myrrh comments.

"Perhaps. Walk with me?"

He hops off the stool, turns, and holds out his hand. She can't help noticing that his arm trembles with hidden emotion. After a moment's hesitation, Myrrh accepts the help down from her stool. They slip out the door and into the predawn light.

Chapter Twenty-Nine

"How long before the city's merchants realize your father is gone?" Myrrh asks.

At their slow pace, it's taken a couple of hours to walk from Rat Town over First Bridge and along the river to where they now stroll beside the waterfront. Neither of them has seemed eager to reach the end of their time together, and the day is now brightening to full morning. So far, the city seems oblivious to the events of the previous night. They're passing through the Crafter's District now, and shop fronts are opening as if nothing has changed. Jewelers, those who work with polished glass and pretty shells rather than the precious gems favored by the merchant class, have set up stalls along the waterfront. One calls out to her, commenting that a smoked-quartz pendant would match her dress.

Glint laughs. "Guess she didn't see the bangle you're already wearing. Worth more than her entire inventory."

"I almost fenced it to help secure enough cargo to make the downriver voyage worthwhile for my new bargemen."

"I meant to ask, where *did* you get the financing?"

"I sold off the rest of the spice."

"My spice," he says, glancing at her sideways.

"Which I stole for you."

"And for that matter, I don't recall giving you possession of the barge."

"But since you didn't explicitly say I *had* to steal the whole vessel, just the cargo aboard it, I'd say ownership of the barge was ambiguous at best."

Abruptly, he grabs her forearm and turns her toward him. Myrrh gasps a little in surprise. Her nerves are still a little frayed, and now she's been more than a day without sleep on top of that.

"Will you reconsider?" he asks, eyes pleading. "Think of the organization we could build. We could even split things up so you run a Rat Town division."

"The new members of Ghost syndicate wouldn't accept it. Not a chance. As it is, I have a major challenge ahead in convincing them that we'll accomplish more when we organize than we did scraping by as solo grubbers."

"You'll really give up what we were accomplishing together in Lower Fringe? Go back to the mud and the tavern brawls and the smell of the water around First Bridge?"

"I suppose I will," she says.

He cups her elbows, then runs the backs of his fingers up her arms. Myrrh shivers.

"The others will be disappointed to hear you're leaving us. They'll blame me for failing to charm you into staying."

His eyes search hers as if desperate for just a hint of weakness. A thinning of her resolve.

"For now, the Rat Town grubbers need me. They deserve the Ghost syndicate." It's the best she can give him. The hint that her choice might not be forever.

"Will you sit with me a little longer? I'm not quite ready to face...everything that needs to be done, I guess." Glint gestures to the low wall that borders the river. Children of the tradespeople in the district gather in small huddles along its length, throwing bits of stale bread to the ducks paddling in the Ost. Myrrh's eyes linger on the closest group as she follows Glint to an empty section of wall. What would her childhood have been like if she'd been able to play instead of picking pockets? How would it feel to remember a mother and father? To have enough food that she could throw some of it to the ducks for fun? She can't even imagine.

Myrrh and Glint sit with their backs to the river, faces to the morning sun.

She closes her eyes and enjoys the warmth. Somewhere in the city, Noble and his henchmen will be having a different experience. The sunrise probably caught them somewhere between the thieves' path under Fourth Bridge and their entrance into Rat Town. Did they shriek when the disk of fire crested the eastern mountains? Did their sudden panic summon the Shield Watch onto them? Or did the pain arrive slowly as dawn washed over the city, leaving them time to find a dark hole to hide out until night?

She should have listened to Glint. Let him set the ambush. They *will* come for her eventually, though their glimmer-blindness will make things more difficult. Except she'd always know she broke her word. She doesn't have much in the world, not now. But at least she still has her integrity.

"I have a question," she says as a cart rattles by, the driver slapping the leads against the horse's back as if to impress any would-be passengers.

"What's that?"

"Lavi."

"What about her?"

"The eye patch."

Glint drops his head back and laughs, hands planted on the wall beneath them. "Why does she wear it when there's nothing wrong with her vision, you mean?"

"With the inlaid gems, I wondered if it was some kind of fashion statement."

"Lavi? Fashion? I believe I let you know what I thought of that nightgown she got you. Though I admit the glimpses I've had of the less...frumpy underthings have forced me to think there's hope for her."

"Not to mention, she picked out this dress with the stupid buttons in the back."

"I do like how it looks on you." He plucks at the layer of fabric over her thigh.

"You just liked having the chance to button me up."

"Actually, I much preferred the unbuttoning..."

Once again, she feels the blush in her cheeks. "So back to the eye patch?"

"Right. Well, she has quite a collection, actually. That was the first time I saw the one with the gems."

"But why?"

"Lavi has...interesting ideas. I can't discount them because she's one of the best skirmishers in the city. She wears the patches one day a week per eye. Apparently, its practice in case she ever loses an eye in a fight."

"I see."

He shrugs. "Like I said, I can't discount her techniques. I guess we won't really know how effective they are unless she actually gets an eye poked out."

Myrrh grimaces. "I sixing hope not. Yuck."

Glint laughs. "Hey, Myrrh?"

She glances over at him. "Yeah?"

Before she can react, his hands are in her hair. His lips press hard against hers. A low sound rises in his throat as the kiss gentles and he parts her lips with his tongue.

Myrrh is paralyzed, her heart thrashing her ribs, her lower belly on fire.

The world fades to nothing but Glint, his lips and hands and his breath on her face.

And then it's over.

He backs away as quickly as he attacked, his fingers untangling from her hair. She opens her eyes. He's staring at her.

Myrrh starts breathing again as her fingertips tingle from lack of air.

"I...that was...unexpected," she says softly.

"Was it? You haven't noticed my interest?"

"Maybe *sudden* would have been a better word."

"I'm used to taking what I want—a thief's prerogative, you know? But it doesn't work that way with you. So I stole what I could before walking away."

"What if I'd have given it freely?"

"You already refused when you made it clear you won't join me in Lower Fringe."

"So you're only interested if I serve beneath you? You don't want someone independent enough to stand on her own?"

Glint's mouth twists in a wry smile. "It's not that at all. But you see, the moment we part ways this morning, you to your syndicate me to my—"

"Your affiliation of villains and burglars?"

He rolls his eyes. "My *organization.* Anyway, the moment we part ways...you know my goals for Ostgard. I've built the first foundations of my criminal empire. We intend to *own* this city someday, and the people I've gathered around me won't settle for anything less. And apparently, your people won't change either." He cups her cheek, rubbing his thumb gently over her skin. "So unless one of us wants to give up our dreams...we're rivals now, Myrrh."

His words sink in, dark clouds pressing over the warmth of the sun. Rivals. Vying for control of a city that's made each of them who they are.

"I thought you weren't into turf wars," she says.

"No. And I don't see you squabbling over boundaries either. I *do* see you building something incredible from the ruins of the Slivers syndicate though. And quite honestly, it terrifies me."

"You, terrified?"

"Ever since I started planning and plotting, I've been confident I'd win in the end. The other syndicates simply aren't a concern. We'll move in, dry up their prospects, and their organizations will slowly and inexorably die. But you represent something different. You're just as clever as me, just as capable, but you think differently. I won't be able to predict you."

It's been so long since she slept. Myrrh's thoughts feel sluggish. The conversation seems almost surreal. She wants to start it over when she's got her wits about her. But Glint is saying there won't be another chance to talk.

He's saying good-bye.

"Will you...will the Scythe still help me free Hawk?"

"Of course, Myrrh. Of course. I'd come with you too, if I didn't have an organization to repair."

"It's hard for me to grasp. You'd give me use of your most loyal soldier even though we're enemies?"

"Not enemies." He touches her wrist. "Never."

"But not friends."

"Hmm. That's complicated. It's not just your capabilities that terrify me, Myrrh. I'm afraid that when the time comes...maybe it will be when you and I are the last kingpins standing...I'm afraid I won't have the strength to hurt you. Because already, part of me wants to abandon everything I've built so I can have another of those kisses. So...friends? I just don't know."

He won't meet her eyes anymore.

Myrrh balls her fists. Not much point in dragging this out then.

"You better go," she says. "Your people are probably pacing the streets with impatience."

He closes his eyes and takes a deep breath. "I'll send the Scythe to Rikson's Roost tomorrow morning. Say hello to Craghold for me. It is my childhood home, after all."

She stands. "Good luck with your play for the council seat. Maybe in a few months you'll be living in the Maire's palace."

"And maybe you'll be taking control of criminal activity along the west bank of the Ost from First Bridge to Fifth."

"Or moving on to plan my conquest of your fading empire."

"We'll see," he says with a wink.

"May the best thief win then?"

She steps back to take in the sight of him looking up at her, clothing rumpled and bruises fading. He may be the most handsome man she's ever met.

"Indeed," he says. "May the best thief win."

Dear Reader,

Thank you so much for reading *Mistress of Thieves.* I really hope you enjoyed it! As a working writer, I utterly depend on readers to spread the word on my books.

Please consider leaving a review on Amazon for this book and for other authors you enjoy. I promise that I read every review (yes, even the critical ones). Sometimes, they help me shape the story to come, and often, they are the reason I get out of bed and in front of my computer long before the sun rises. Thank you!!

If you would like to grab free books and participate in my reader community, head over to www.CarrieSummers.com and join my reader group. We have a lot of fun writing collaborative stories over email, talking about books, and other great stuff. Plus, the group is how I let readers know when new books are out.

So, what's next? *Ruler of Scoundrels* is the second book in this series. Look for it on Amazon! And while you're there, you can check out my other series, *The Shattering of the Nocturnai* and *The Broken Lands.*

Once again, thank you for reading!

All best,

—Carrie

carrie@carriesummers.com

PS. Check after the acknowledgements for a preview of *Ruler of Scoundrels!*

*Acknowledgements*

I'd like to thank my husband, Dave, for his tireless support. Lindsey Nelson of Exact Edits did a wonderful job with the manuscript. And thanks to all my readers for supporting me so I can keep doing this!

Ruler of Scoundrels
Chapter One

STREWN ACROSS A table in The Queen's Dice, shards of glass twinkle in the lamplight. A dark pool of blood spreads across the battered floorboards. Myrrh can't help staring at the stain, its sticky surface marred by a single footprint. The urchin they sent to fetch her said that no one died. Just a bad knife slash to a man's arm. Looking at the mess, she has a hard time believing that.

After a deep breath, she turns to the mistress of the house. Sapphire, a sturdy woman with a raised scar across her chin, stands behind one of her dealers, a hand on his shoulder. Her eyes are hard. Uncompromising. This violence happened under Myrrh's watch. In Ghost syndicate turf. It's Myrrh's responsibility.

Myrrh closes her mind to the smell of blood and hardens her jaw. "You should probably get that cleaned up before it dries."

Sapphire narrows her eyes. "You needed to see what happened here."

The woman's tone is just short of defiant. Myrrh feels her nostrils flare, and she forces her hands into her pockets to show the proprietor she won't be intimidated. She edges around the blood and steps toward a wall where a wrought-iron symbol dedicated to the Queen of Nines hangs askew. From across the room, she feels the stares of the dealers and the bartender. They're pretending to be interested in a game of dice.

"I assure you I'm capable of understanding a report without being subjected to the grisly scene. You do realize I came into leadership of the Ghost syndicate by skill rather than chance, don't you?"

"However you gained control of the turf isn't my concern. The welfare of my business establishment is."

Myrrh sighs as she turns. "Why don't you start by telling me what happened?"

Sapphire hesitates, off-balanced by Myrrh's sudden change of tone. After years of working with the Slivers syndicate, she's probably more used to threats than being asked for her side of the story.

Myrrh calls across the room to the bartender. "Hey, can you get us an ale and whatever Sapphire is drinking? On me."

He blinks as if unsure.

"Or do I need to do it myself?" Myrrh prompts.

The man's chair squeals as he pushes back from the dice game. Returning her attention to Sapphire, Myrrh gestures toward an empty table, eyebrows raised in question. After a moment, the proprietor nods. They pull out chairs and sit in tense silence until the drinks arrive, a pewter mug with overflowing foam for Myrrh and a modest tumbler of whiskey for Sapphire. Myrrh drops a silver piece on the table, the coin settling with a click. The bartender's practiced hand sweeps it away.

Sapphire lays two fingers on the bartender's arm before he walks away. She flicks her eyes toward the spilled blood. "You can start on that now. Fetch Becky to help."

The man rounds the bar and pushes through a swinging door that squeals as it opens. His gruff voice echoes in the back rooms. Meanwhile, the dealers—five in total—lean close to one another and whisper over the dicing table. One, a woman, glances at Myrrh with open curiosity while a man with slicked-back hair glares her way.

"The rest of you scat," Sapphire calls.

They hesitate until their boss lays hands on the table and threatens to stand. With disappointed snorts, they abandon their game. More glass crunches under their feet as they file through the room to the back door. Once they're outside, Sapphire gets up and drops the bar into place before returning to her seat.

"It's been a decade since someone was knifed in my establishment," she says bluntly. "I never liked Slivers' methods, but I can't argue with their results."

Myrrh takes a swallow of her ale, sets the mug on the table with a clack. "And you blame me."

Sapphire shrugs, allowing Myrrh to draw her own conclusions. Myrrh studies a line of foam sliding down her mug as she considers her response. Should she attempt to defend herself? Ask questions? Either option would make her look weak and inept. She decides to hold her silence.

The bartender returns, trailed by a wan-faced scullery maid—Becky, no doubt—who blanches at the sight of the blood. Ignoring her hesitation, the bartender drops a set of rags over the rapidly drying blood. He raises an eyebrow at Becky. The girl swallows and falls to her knees beside the bucket she carried into the room.

For a while, the only sounds in the room are the splash of water and the scratching of the scrub brush's bristles. The bartender stands over the girl, monitoring her work and occasionally stepping behind the bar for more clean rags.

Finally, the proprietor of the gambling den snorts in amusement. Myrrh blinks, not sure what about the situation is funny.

"All right, you got me. I had to test your mettle, see what the new boss of Rat Town is made of. But no, I don't blame you for what happened here. Your men performed well. Got the fight stopped before anyone got killed. And considering the situation, that was quite a feat."

"Ghost syndicate doesn't have a strict hierarchy," Myrrh says.

Sapphire's brows draw together while she runs a finger around the rim of her glass. The smell of wet wood impregnated with years of spilled liquor rises from the floor and finally starts to overpower the stench of blood.

"Not sure I follow your change of subject," the proprietor says.

"You called me the boss of Rat Town. Said the security assigned to your establishment were 'my men'. But the syndicate's decisions are made by a council, not a single person."

"Well, claim what you will. According to everyone I've heard tell it, there's only one person calling the shots in your new syndicate."

Myrrh takes another swallow of her beer and wonders if she should ask why no one's helping poor Becky.

"But I didn't send Wren to fetch you just so I could see your reaction," Sapphire says.

"Wren?"

"The little orphan girl."

Right. The urchin. "So what *is* this about then?"

Becky casts a nervous glance in their direction, prompting the bartender to nudge her hip with his toe. She jerks, nearly knocking into the bucket of red water. Myrrh takes a deep breath.

"In case you're wondering," Sapphire says, "I caught Becky here pinching coins from one of the tables. The way I see it, my patrons have a right to enjoy their gaming without being pickpocketed. Especially when the thief is lucky to have honest work under my roof. But we've all made mistakes at one time or another, isn't that right, Becky?"

"Yes, Mistress," the girl says as she scrubs harder.

Sapphire smirks and winks at Myrrh. "In any case, I didn't send for you just because there was a brawl. It's about *who* came looking for the fight. And why. The Queen's Dice had a prior arrangement with the Slivers syndicate, as I'm sure you're aware. I admit to being surprised to see Noble back here. Especially given his new...condition."

Noble. The former leader of the Slivers syndicate. Yeah, Myrrh can see why his reappearance might cause problems.

"So it's true?" Myrrh says. "He's a White? I never got confirmation."

"If by that, you mean blinded by glimmer in all but the dimmest light...eyes shining silver.... Yeah. I'd say he's a White."

"I expected him to turn up in Rat Town eventually," Myrrh says. "Sorry it brought trouble to your establishment."

Sapphire shrugs. "Long as you make it right with extra security until he's been dealt with, we're good."

Myrrh keeps her face even. It was hard enough to find thieves willing to take on security gigs across the district. As former freelancers, the members of Ghost syndicate are accustomed to heists and smuggling and blackmail. Jobs with a bit of excitement and chance at surprise payouts. In comparison, the steady percentage take from gambling house profits will buy food and ale, but no one will be founding an empire on the sums.

When Slivers controlled the territory, it was simpler. Syndicate members didn't have a choice in their assignments, and they received fixed stipends from the syndicate coffers no matter their work. But that's not the sort of organization Myrrh founded.

"It will be hard to find the muscle unless you're willing to contribute a larger percentage."

Sapphire's eyes narrow, but Myrrh holds firm. She's pretty sure the proprietor's spending half of what she did under Noble's organization.

"I could increase the allowance as long as the situation is temporary," Sapphire says after a moment.

"Then I'll figure it out. So...I'm guessing Noble had some grievances to air."

Sapphire snorts. "Yeah, you could say that."

"Well, I didn't expect him to hide out in the dark forever."

"He was throwing around a lot of nasty threats. I'd be wary if I were you. Noble still has heavy support in this district. Lots of thieves and sellswords lost their livelihoods when you ousted Slivers."

"They're welcome to work for Ghost syndicate as long as they agree to our rules."

"I'm not the audience you need to reach with that message," Sapphire says.

"No, probably not."

Sapphire traces a finger across the wood grain on the table. "The way you talk about the syndicate, I'm not surprised people call you the boss. It's clear you make most of the decisions."

Myrrh doesn't respond. A cool swallow of ale slides down her throat.

"Anyway, when Noble started mentioning a bounty for your head, that's when blades came out. I'll give you credit. He might have support after so many years running Rat Town, but you have your own loyalists. A shift worker from the smelters took a nasty slash to the arm when he threatened one of Noble's lackeys. That's when your security stepped in started throwing the Slivers crew out the door."

"How many were there?"

"Five, counting Noble."

"Any others glimmer-blind?"

Sapphire shakes her head. "Just the kingpin. He wears a hat low over his eyes. Can't seem to look directly at candles without pain. I'm not surprised he's got a vendetta."

Myrrh takes a deep breath. Maybe she should have listened to Glint and ambushed the Slivers leadership before they learned she'd slipped them a glimmer overdose and taken over their turf. But that would have meant going against her word. Sometimes, details mattered.

The reminder of Glint brings a tightness to her chest that eases when she takes another deep drink of ale. No doubt he would have good advice on how to deal with Noble's reemergence. Probably delivered close to her ear in a low voice. She grits her teeth at the involuntary shiver that travels her spine at the thought.

She really needs to avoid distractions like that. She has a syndicate to run. Kids like Nab need her protection, especially with the city trembling in fear over the turmoil in Maire's Quarter. Plus, she has to figure out what's going on with Hawk. Why he came out of Craghold so…changed.

And right now, she's got to conclude business with Sapphire and The Queen's Dice. Ideally followed by a nice date with her pillow.

"You comfortable with my people denying Noble entry tomorrow night?" she asks.

Sapphire slugs back the last of her whiskey. "Please."

"The guards will be here at dusk then."

"There's another thing," Sapphire says.

"Oh?"

"A man. Never seen him before. He spoke to me once things quieted down."

"What about him?"

"He said he wanted me to give you a message."

"Another threat?"

"I don't think so. He came from downriver. Some place called Glenhaven."

"It's about halfway between here and the sea."

"If you say so," Sapphire says with a shrug. "Anyway, he heard of Ghost syndicate and was, as he said, intrigued. He wants to talk to you."

"Like I said earlier, anyone who wants to abide by the syndicate rules is welcome to work for us. We send word through the taverns every evening. New gigs and what they pay."

"I think he's looking for more than a few jobs. He asked if you would meet him here tomorrow. Around midnight."

"If he's interested in the syndicate, he can ask any Ghost member. I'm sure plenty of them enjoy throwing the dice at your tables."

Sapphire presses her lips together. "If you don't mind me saying, the man had an air about him. Seemed to be more than a common thief. I'd figure out what he's about if I were you."

The woman's serious tone grabs Myrrh's attention. She gets the sense Sapphire wouldn't keep pressing if she didn't feel it was important.

"In that case, no, I don't mind you saying. And I'll try to be here."

Myrrh plants her palms on the table and stands. Before she can leave the table, Sapphire touches on her wrist. "Then I'll drop you another bit of honest advice. You shouldn't walk around Rat Town this late alone."

Myrrh shrugs. "I've never had a problem."

The silence stretches out while Myrrh works Sapphire's words over.

"Look," Sapphire says, "I don't know you well enough to care one way or the other. But I *do* care about Rat Town. Regardless of Slivers' flaws, they kept order around here. Don't kid yourself into thinking Ghost syndicate would hang together without you. They'd collapse the moment you got knifed in an alley. Leaving us in a much worse situation than we had before. So if you care about anyone down here and want to see them live until next Rhemmsfest, stop being careless."

After a moment, Myrrh sighs. "Fair enough. Got anyone who could escort me to my residence?"

Sapphire casts her a crooked smile. “We secure more bets in a night than any gambling house in Rat Town. Think I sit on that much coin without plenty of my own muscle to guard it?”

The woman nods toward one of the walls. No doubt catching the eye of someone at a hidden peephole.

“Someone will meet you outside,” she says.

Made in the USA
San Bernardino, CA
20 January 2020

63416334R00168